MW00685004

QUEEN GODSHEREN REIGNS

By

Emmanuel S. Goka

Shield Crest

ISBN 978-1-912505-51-7

MMXIX

A CIP catalogue record for this book is available from the British Library

Published by
ShieldCrest
Aylesbury, Buckinghamshire, HP18 0TF
England
www.shieldcrest.co.uk
+44 (0) 333 8000 890

Dedication

To Aku Ethel Selormey for your intuitive knowledge in getting me to put on your personal cover cloth (instead of the suit I had worn) prior to walking through the road of death which, again by intuition, you knew I was going to walk. I knew nothing about such a walk and returned unscathed avoiding that certain death to anyone who walks that road.

I dedicate to you the fictional novel, 'Queen Godsheren Reigns '.

A story about a non-royal girl who rejected and mocked a man who proposed romantic love to her, but she accepted his gift. She then onwards led a life of promiscuity by becoming an alternate wife to every husband of every wife in the city that was eventually named after her. She, years later, became the lawful wife of three husbands, but two of the husbands deserted her. And with one husband left, through happenstance, she was crowned as queen of the city and kingdom that bore her name and, to that one kingdom, were added four other kingdoms and she ruled over all as one unified kingdom.

Queen Godsheren introduced new insights and ideas, implemented policies and carried out actions and services in her kingdom that should be the benchmark for future kings and queens, possibly for nation or country heads or presidents, or to measure or judge past kings or queens.

Queen Godsheren gave a new working definition of what it means to be coronated as king or queen.

CONTENTS

CHAPTER 1

ENO DUA

Philadelphia, PA, USA
July 24, 2018

Under the main directional sign to the Centre City is the only small neon directional arrow pointing in the opposite direction of Eno Dua ('breasts city' it means in our mother tongue). We drove to the Centre City and checked in to our hotel rooms. We ate lunch, that was not soft on our pockets, rested some hours and then all three of us, out of curiosity, decided to visit the breasts city in the opposite direction to the Centre City.

We arrived and were about to drive through a passageway to enter Eno Dua when a security man asked us to return because it was closing time. He therefore shut the gate in our faces. Surprised, we wondered if this was 'Eno Dua' as we'd simply translated the words from our mother tongue into English. It could mean many things in different languages. It depends who the reader is.

We looked at each other in the face, and Dalina asked us, the other two men, "Boo and Dabi, is it fair to translate any words in your mother tongue into English that you see or read in any foreign country that you travel to, and that doesn't speak that language, the travellers' mother tongue?"

I realized he had a point, but asked him to wait till we got back to the hotel.

When we got back to the hotel, sleep took the better part of us, none of us raised the question Dalina raised earlier, and we went to our various rooms; not even 'Za ne nenyo. Do agbe' ('Good night, sleep, and rise alive') did we say to each other.

And though we didn't speak words of safety into the night, our desires for it not to take away our lives during its hours of operation (night) were realized. It, the night, 'handed' us to the day and its daylight hours, and at breakfast we spoke into the day and asked for life and success at everything.

We spoke simultaneously after breakfast of our going to visit Eno Dua, though that was not on the itinerary for the first day after arrival day (the previous day).

Dalina, who was to receive a chemotherapy treatment for blood cancer, alongside being a speaker at the conference that we all were to attend the following five days, spoke saying, "When two mouths speak simultaneously, there is certainty that the day will offer the best of what they spoke about. But when three mouths speak simultaneously, the god of the place where the people spoke is directing their lives."

We soon got to the Eno Dua gate in our hired car. The security man, who recognized us, said, "When a gate is locked in your face once, it makes you not to have any more gates locked in your face. Please, who is sick among you?" he asked.

Surprised at his question, Dalina and Dabi simultaneously asked, "Is it a hospital? Or a prayer healing centre?"

"It is Eno Dua; a restorative place for those who cannot be healed at hospitals and prayer healing centres. Only the sick person can enter. No other person is allowed," the security guard said.

So we thought, and I answered, "If it is a restorative centre or whatever, sir, then whether you know you are sick or not, you can go in, and when you are restored you will know you were sick but didn't know."

"That is a good answer. You've just expanded our business horizon. I am the business development manager and will add that line – not determined as sick or diseased – to our line of business. You should have paid before entry, but you definitely must be honest men and will pay when you notice you are restored," the business development manager said.

He pressed an electric knob and the gate slid to one side and, at the parking lot, Dalina, forgetting that we were out of hearing range of him, whispered, "Not every gatekeeper in the technology world is a security guard. Very soon, even CEOs will be gatekeepers."

"Ah! Dalina, Why in whispers? Facts are facts. We noted our error when he described his status. And we took that on board," Dabi said.

"Well, electronic hearing aids could have picked more than whisperings and transmitted the wrong message of what I said. And we could spend the conference days defending ourselves against belittling a fella," Dalina explained.

In the grounds of Eno Dua we saw ten scattered but big houses (what looked like dwelling homes), green lawns, and a large square flower garden around each building with only paved access or egress.

I, Boo, pressed the buzzer on the front door. It opened, then another door opened, and we were in a large open room with wall-to-wall mirrors on all sides.

A woman, twenty-eight-ish by her looks, entered, dressed up to a little above her navel, and there was a kick in our bodies and we retreated backwards at the significant exposed top of her body, but nevertheless smiled, when we regained our composure.

With a radiating smile, she said "Welcome." She explained that there were two restorative rooms in each house: the natural breasts restorative room, manned by six women of varying ages and with different types of breasts, where a focus on each woman's breasts for thirty minutes times six (women) would give a restorative total age of sixty years backwards (health wellbeing); the second room she described as the 'mirror breasts room' that has one natural woman's breasts and five mirror images of her breasts. The focus time in the second room was the same. "And, please, your election or no election," she explained, and mentioned her name as Anita, stating, "My true name,"

Dalina spoke first and said, "I will do both."

And not knowing what was wrong or right with us, Dabi and I also answered, "Both."

"Then you could use houses 1, 2 and 3's facilities," Anita suggested. "And who goes to house 2 and who to house 3?" she asked.

"Dalina remains in house 1, Dali to house 2, and I, Boo, to house 3," I answered her.

One hundred and eighty minutes later, Anita's voice sounded asking, "Would you take a break for fifteen to thirty minutes and continue your focused looking?"

"Ah, no, no," we three simultaneously said.

"Are you brothers?" she asked.

"Work companions," we again simultaneously said.

"That is long and true friendship, and therefore able to speak simultaneously," Anita said.

And it was after another one hundred and eighty minutes that we heard her voice again.

We paid and drove back to our hotel.

"Anyone feeling hungry?" Dalina asked.

"No to your question," the two of us answered.

"I am also not hungry," Dalina answered. "Then to the cancer centre," he requested.

After three hours of tests, the specialist told him there were no cancer cells in his blood, and no need for even drug treatment, more so, chemotherapy. Dalina paid, without our telling the specialist what we did at Eno Dua.

We were the happiest threesome at the conference all five days and made many interventions, so much so that the two professors, the resource persons, invited us to join them in writing a new textbook, the first time any other person or persons were accorded that honour.

On the flight back home, when we saw anyone with exposed breasts, we knew the person didn't know what she has and the value thereof.

We are working on a book on, *The Economic Potential of the Exposed Breasts*, but, unfortunately, we have signed a confidentiality agreement with Eno Dua and cannot disclose the six types of breasts that will put all types of healing practitioners out of business, except the breasts healers.

The two professors have read our book, but is yet to be launched. The professors have advised that we write a sequel and, when that is completed, we will have two bestsellers instead of one because billions of women will buy the books, and even more men than women.

Eno Dua offers what it says: 'First restorative visit permanently restores health and wellness.'

We are witnesses. And our testimonials in the two books will change the world of humans.

CHAPTER 2

TOO MANY 'AMENS'

Philadelphia, PA, USA
July 25, 2018

I waited at the Rotunda House Food Court for hours because the rainy weather, surprisingly for summer this year, wouldn't stop, and I didn't have a raincoat that would be the right fit for the pouring rain, or an umbrella that would pretend to be covering me from the rain I shielded myself from. And with no interest or appetite for the various dishes that contained more salt and sugar than vegetables and fish or meat and varied carbohydrates combined, my hunger pains made the hours seem twice the time lapse.

Additionally, the few clothing stores on the floor below the Food Court floor couldn't occupy my mind and legs through walking and window-shopping because they sold only feminine stuff. And my going into such shops and being seen by even a ghost, perchance looking at any of the items that give some women added but removable beauty, could be misinterpreted by the 'ghost' visitor from my village as purchasing for those not in the village but in this, my temporary place of residence. And the inference will be whether in the village, or in the foreign country, I have a harem of women, and therefore have been seen in women's clothing stores.

I was relieved when the rain stopped. I went to the big mall that I always shop in because of their return policy, and the grant to visitors of additional discount with no eye of distrust (moreover the mind) following you because of the colour of your

6

skin and possibly your blood. Very soon, some of their scientists will say the blood type within humans determines their skin colour. I stopped in front of the elevator station. They had four in all.

There stood a middle-aged woman in front of the elevators to board an elevator upwards to any of the higher floors of the thirteen-story mall. I walked and stood by her. She looked down, as if in prayer to her feet, when one of the many elevators stopped at the ground floor. She boarded, and I also did. I was surprised that, with the milling crowds in the mall, only she and I boarded, when the escalators were not working, and shoppers were not using the staircases.

She coughed and bent over double. I hoped she wasn't going to die and I be accused of killing her, since security operatives operate on the basis that the opportunistic individual (the nearest or closest to you in location or time) should be the first suspect and be questioned and or arrested. But she started praying, (so I thought and was relieved), and continued till the elevator stopped at the twelfth floor. When the elevator doors opened, and she was stepping out, I nearly said 'Amen' in response to her prayers, but my hand cupped my mouth.

I got out on the thirteenth floor, because I was looking for home furnishings and that was the floor for them. I picked a few things, paid, and went home.

Next day, having slept through the night without a body touching or caressing me, and not even a dream of romance to carry me through the daylight hours, I decided to go visit a few other places. I was twenty kilometres away from my temporary home, but nearly one hundred kilometres from the mall I visited the previous day, when a police car I passed by on the opposite side of the street kept persistently buzzing every second. I felt something was amiss. The policeman in the parked car got out, and crossed over to my side of the street.

"I will have to arrest you for a crime of indecent assault on an old lady," he said.

"Where was that?" I asked.

"In an elevator within the Meridian Super Mall," he answered.

"Seriously? Not a case of mistaken identity?" I asked.

"Please, you must not say anything and you need not say anything because whatever you say will be recorded and could be used against you. You are entitled to a criminal attorney before giving you statement," he advised. "You will have to accompany me to the precincts," he said.

"Can I come in my hired car? I have an aversion to sitting in police cars from my teenage years because of a story I heard. A priest and priestess died when someone told them that their son was in a police car," I asked and explained.

He mumbled something, and said, "Your parents won't die, because no one will see you in a police car and tell them, and because you are in another country, not in your home country. We have a copy of the visitor's card you used when you purchased."

The mall HR was at the precinct when we got there. She came along with the video CCTV recording of the particular day and of two days earlier.

The middle-aged woman who was in the elevator the previous day alongside me looked truly like an elderly woman at the precinct. I sat in a chair quietly, knowing that technology – two different types, the CCTV video and the related audio recordings – and DNA would exclude or exonerate me from the alleged crime. It was only that the wait was ten hours long.

"Suspect/accused and victim/accuser both waste time. There is no suspect/accused in this case. No such incident happened for a question of mistaken identity to arise," Dinggong, the policeman, said.

"I am free to leave?" I asked.

And as I was leaving, with the knowledge that I have no mother or father to die from seeing photos on social media, she was looking glamorously beautiful. She had changed from an old lady to one many years less than a middle-aged woman.

When I told my story on my return home to my village church members, the village catechist said, "Too many people are saying loud 'amens' when 'amens' must be valued. If you know what the 'amen' is and know its value, you will say it as a response to only your prayer at home or in temples, but not in trains or airplanes, no, not in any other place other than the two."

CHAPTER 3

BE CAREFUL THE WATERS

Philadelphia, PA, USA
July 26, 2018

Whil Indora and Lindora, the two women, stopped in their walk along the Watutu coast, on its sandy beaches for us (Boo, Dalina and Dabi), to pass by before they continued their walk, a flashing heat (like the sun's rays) and a light (like the moon's brightness) went through us a minute apart.

We turned and looked back at them to see if they would also turn and look in our direction. They also turned and, looking in our direction, smiled, followed by giggles.

Then we saw their eyes blinking with a brightness that could not come out of a human eye but gods or goddesses. We fell prostrate and bowed our heads to touch the sand, twice each.

When we raised our heads up, there was no sight of them. And I, Boo, said, "If we have found favour in their sight, having done obeisance to them acknowledging that they are gods (goddesses), they will appear to us again in not more than a distance of two miles."

"We will continue walking for as long as possible. For it is only those who don't want the blessings of the gods that will retreat in fear and not wish to have a second meeting, or crossing of paths, when the gods will ask us as to what we want or wish, and, on our answering them, will grant us multiples of blessings. I have suffered the past two years when I went through another baptism. I don't know what I was baptized into. I must meet the gods a second time for a possible answer," Dalina said.

"Ah! You didn't know that Boo and I also went through another baptism?" Dabi asked.

"Oh! You did?" Dalina asked.

And I answered, and stated, "We were baptized into a human being, a living being, not a dead being, for if it was a dead being, it will be an ancestor, and be part of the crowd of witnesses the Christian Church speaks about. The living being that I know is the head pastor of the church; it is him whom we have been baptized into. It was 'his' baptism, not that of John the Baptist, not that of Jesus Christ. Because, the words, 'In the name of God, the Father; God, the Son; and God, the Holy Spirit' was not mentioned."

"Hahaha! There are many fathers and many gods, and we should have been careful in choosing into whose name we were or are baptized," Dalina said, and immediately also said, "I have heard shuffling sounds ahead of us. It could not be that of the fishermen who ply their trade in the seawaters and mend their nets and rest on the sandy beaches."

"I can also hear," I said.

And a minute later, Dabi said, "I see two women ahead, facing each other as if playing a game with the sand."

"Ah-ooh!" the two others expressed.

"They are playing a game. When you see gods (goddesses) playing a game know they are happy and will bless whoever sees them," Boo and Dalina simultaneously said.

You cannot walk stealthily to surprise gods at play. We knew they knew we had seen them. We reached where (the spot) they were playing the game.

With a shout of "Ayekoo" from all three of us, they turned to the direction our voices came from.

"I am Indira. And my sister is Lindora," the first to speak said.

"And we are Boo, Dabi and Dalina," Dabi introduced us.

"And what brings you to the sandy beaches?" Indira asked.

"We love walking. The exercise of walking," I answered.

"That is a game of walking. If you walk alone it is an exercise. But if you walk with others, it is not only an individual exercise but also a game. And if you play a game with a woman, or women, they offer only what a woman or women can offer: contentment," Indira explained.

And Lindora, speaking for the first time, said, "When you play with gods (goddesses), whether you recognize them or not, they will offer you the blessings of gods. Will you play with us?"

"Wow! It would be a joy and pleasure to play with you two," we three men answered.

Then Indira cupped sand in both hands and threw it into our eyes, blinding each of us.

"Eh! Have I hurt you? Did the sand enter your eyes? she asked.

"The sand entered our eyes. But we are not blinded or hurt. But rather, we see better and clearer," each of the men individually said.

"And what do you each see?" Lindora asked.

"I see the sun, but the sun looks like Indira. And Indira also looks like the sun. Indira has merged into the sun and I see only a circular sun," I said in answer.

"And us, Dabi And Dalina, have seen exactly what Boo has described. And we have seen Lindora looking like the moon and the moon looking like Lindora. Lindora has merged into the moon and we see a circular moon. We are certain Boo has seen the moon, as Lindora and Lindora are like the moon, with Lindora merging into the circular moon and only the circular moon remaining," Dabi and Dalina explained.

"You will be blessed with all daytime blessings that you ask for in the name of Indira," Indira said.

"You will also be blessed with all night blessings you ask for in the name of Lindora," Lindora said.

"Be careful into whose name you make your requests and therefore bow your head in reverence through baptism," both Indira and Lindora advised.

"The Earth is the Lord's and the Lord is the Earth. And the Lord is the sun to rule by day and the moon to rule by night. In bowing our heads to touch the earth in obeisance, the sun and moon do jointly bless us with the various gifts we ask for," we three men said, one after the other. and we saw no more the two women, Indira and Lindora, but the sun and moon, but remembered Indira and Lindora.

Then we returned home and continually took walks by day and walks by night.

CHAPTER 4

UNLESS YOU ARE KEPT . . . AND WHAT MEAL?

Philadelphia, PA, USA
July 28, 2018

On the night Godsheren turned fifteen years of age, she left home every night without her parent's knowledge and/or consent. And throughout that first night, her parents heard intermittent hissing sounds and the first four hours affected their sleep. They reasoned that the many types of snakes that come from their habitation during the hot and dry summer months looking for cooler places, such as, bedrooms and washrooms, had taken sleeping places in the washroom. They both went to look with two different lanterns, one white and the other red coloured, so that if the white light didn't enable them to see any reptile, the red light would attract any reptile in the bathroom. And finding none, and having eaten a hot pepper meal that makes for deep sleep, (once the meal is no longer in the chest area (large intestine)), they fell into a deep sleep and both missed their 5am early morning chores; the mother to rise up to sweep the compound, and the father to go to the farm and uproot the weeds that would be competing with tomato and okra crops.

Godsheren was busily washing her and the parent's clothing when the mother walked into the kitchen to prepare breakfast. The mother exchanged pleasantries with her and expressed that, "Godsheren, you look more beautiful than your mother when she was your age."

To which compliment, Godsheren responded, "If your mother is beautiful, and she is the daughter of a beautiful mother,

her daughter (Godsheren) will be three times more beautiful than her mother. And Godsheren has her grandmother's and yours, her (mother's) beauty in addition to her own beauty."

"Anyway Godsheren, that doesn't mean with three beauties rolled into one person, you will have three husbands," the mother said.

"Mother, can I say something?" Godsheren asked.

"Why not, my daughter? A mother who answers her daughter's questions makes the daughter to become a better mother, and her mother receives the honour of her future husband, he building a house with only diverse flowers for her. Your question, Godsheren," the mother asked.

"Hmm! How about three husbands? I am three times beautiful," Godsheren asked.

"Ah! Ha-ha!! You can't be three mothers. It is with the first child's birth that you are a mother. Any other children don't change your status. And the men are not even enough to go around all women," the mother answered her, and left her when Godsheren asked no other question.

Godsheren did all the daytime chores and, when night fell, she left home again without her parent's knowledge.

And for the second night, the regular intermittent hissing sounds were heard. But this second night they also heard, faintly, a few seconds' humming sounds with deep breathing intermittently.

But the parents slept with the thought that the few seconds of the faint humming sounds with deep breathing could be coming from the immediate next-door neighbour's bedroom, and nobody checks on sounds from a neighbour's bedroom because yours, which could have been louder, they complained not about.

And every day for three years, Godsheren ate not meals cooked at home during the daytime hours. But with her growth spurts, not showing any retardation, and facial appearance and body looking glamorous every new day, the parents assumed she was picking at the food mostly at home in the kitchen and also weight watching.

Emmanuel S. Goka

And it was no coincidence that a man from outside their country arrived, saw Godsheren's beauty, and within two weeks she was married to him. He enjoyed the hissing sound times with her, that happened when they were having sexual intercourse. And he loved the night times. They later changed to daytime also, of having sexual intercourses, because the husband was due to travel back to the country he came from. And so at night or day, the hissing sounds continued during sexual intercourse, and the parents still heard that in addition to the humming sounds with intermittent deep breathing.

The husband's time being up to travel back to his post, he went to inform his in-laws. And that night, Godsheren's as husband was departing by air, scarcely had he boarded the aircraft then the hissing sounds bombarded him. He felt elated, because whether present physically or absent in body, he could enjoy the sounds he had begun to cherish at night and at day and therefore relate to the wife. At his destination, he had the good fortune six thousand miles away of the hissing sounds and his continuing happiness both night and day.

But that changed when he began to hear humming sounds with deep breathing intermittently also, and then there would be a break followed by another round of hissing sounds and humming sounds with deep breathing.

And from afar, he accused her of infidelity. She agreed. He rued the day he married her. But he refused to divorce her, hoping that any time he came to the country, Godsheren would offer him the hissing sounds and the humming sounds with the deep breathing because his four weeks of every year of intimate times with her as husband were the best, in comparison to his twenty years of a failed marriage.

But she declined his request when he came on a visit and moved onto many hundreds of men in her coastal city. And within years, many thousands of men (including the chief of her city), all the men except the impotent, had heard her hissing sounds and the humming sounds with deep breathing.

16

The chief's counsellors, having heard of the inexpressible joys of the men who had sexual relations with Godsheren and confirmed by the chief, made a decision that Godsheren shall be the alternative wife to all wives (a wife of all men) because of the wonder and amazement associated with her.

Godsheren's name, but not photos, were published on social media when the decision by the chief's counsellors was publicly announced, and all other women were informed that she was a 'protected' woman; you touch or insult her at your peril, as you will be tied with a rope and thrown into the sea.

Having read the news on a particular Tuesday morning, I was shocked when Dalina and Dabi came over to me with information that evening that our book, *The Economic Potential of the Exposed Breasts*, would be launched by the publishers in the 'Godsheren city', as they jokingly mentioned.

"Why go to a lioness's den? Is it to play with her or tease her?" I asked.

The other two gave me no answer; but looked as if meditating. I didn't press them for an answer.

At night, the moon shone brightly in our various bedrooms as if there were no curtains blocking the moon's brightness on a dark night, and we each, the following morning, learnt this through conversation.

And all three of us, with the moon 'incident' behind us, travelled to Godsheren City for the launch which took place, and we partied late into the night, retiring to our hotel rooms just on the hour tick of midnight.

With so many of the book sold, (bought by women who don't expose their breasts from what the publishers said), the publishers asked that we stay for additional six-day vacation so that women and possibly men from the neighbouring communities could also come and buy.

We agreed, possibly with the hope that we could hear more from the men about Godsheren and the difference she makes, or hope that each of us also would be fortunate to have her pay us a surprise visit individually to our rooms, so as to experience the

'Godsheren difference' that made a chief and his counsellors decide that she (one woman) shall be an alternative wife to all men. Nothing like that had been heard of in any country on Earth before.

But was the Indira and Lindora meeting any different from hers, if we should meet her? She also could be one of the planets in the universe, as Indira and Lindora are respectively the sun and the moon, I reasoned in my mind, and reasoned further that the other two were going through the same brain exercise as me, not that they 'could', because I know men, but what that they 'would' want to experience it for themselves, more so, when it does not kill or maim but gives pleasure.

And therefore, when I heard a knock on my room door at 1am, I opened it at that time of the night, hopeful that it would be Godsheren but not a hotel worker.

She walked into the hotel room not wearing hotel clothing.

"Godsheren, it is you. What a pleasant but expectant surprise," I said.

She went for the bed. She laid on it and took off her outer dress.

I fell asleep, and when I woke up the following morning at 5am, she asked, "Were you sick? And how come the moon streamed into the room when the curtains were closed and lights in the room switched off? And not only that, it kept restraining me from getting close to you."

"Please, another night will explain the mystery. I was actually expectant, as I informed you earlier," I explained, and she took her handbag and left me alone.

At all the three meals times of that day, I didn't tell the two others of what happened, though they both hoped that Godsheren would pay them a surprise visit.

And so it was that another night fell, and I was on alert for the knock on the door. At two hours before midnight, I coincidentally opened the door, and she entered. She went to the washroom, changed into a nightie and sat by me on the bed.

The next morning, she said, "It has happened again. Everything I said to you after the first night."

With a mouth tongue-tied, it was only after she left the room that I mentioned her name, saying, "I have slept on the same bed with Godsheren, but not her body touched . . ." But I couldn't complete the sentence as I heard the voices of the others asking that we go to the breakfast area.

I again kept quiet about the visit of Godsheren and had no more expectation of a third night's visit, or her return for a daytime visit, having failed her twice.

But my expectation was that she would visit the other two and they would also either fail or succeed.

On the morning of the eighth day, we checked out for our return journey. We were all quiet till halfway through the distance, when Dalina said, "My friends, how come the coastal men succeeded with Godsheren? Two nights in succession, I failed her."

"I have also failed," Dabi simply said.

"I also failed, where you have failed. But my thoughts tell me that Godsheren is a snake and also a woman. That is why she hisses as a snake, and hums sounds with deep breathing as a woman, and eats as food spermatozoa. Lindora, my apologies! The moon prevented us . . ." I answered, not completing the sentence.

CHAPTER 5

WHAT VALUE YOUR MOUTH;
WHAT VALUE YOUR HAND

Philadelphia, PA, USA
July 29, 2018

W e heard the voices and cries of many women in our
sleep every night since our return from the Godsheren
coastal city. And, each morning, we tried to discuss
how many voices and cries of how many women each of us heard.

"It was as many as the seconds in the sleeping hours of the
night," each of us would answer.

A month went by and there was no respite. But added to the
voices and cries of all those women, was the flagging of the name,
'Godsheren' every minute and persistently before our eyes from
then onwards. And so our eyes and ears were occupied while we
slept and we couldn't hear any other voice or cry or see any other
person, not even our wives or children while we slept.

We continued to discuss and give thought to the happenings
of the nights. As regards Godsheren's name flagging every
minute, none of us felt anything mentally, emotionally,
romantically or sexually towards her, except revulsion that one
woman would cause tears in many homes, though not of her
direct making as she didn't compel the women's husbands to
make her an alternate wife.

And if the reports we received from the coastal city after our
return were anything to go by, no husband ever desired his wife
after a time with Godsheren, and those women didn't find any
value in continuing to work and live.

When we were reminded of these two factors by one of such women, who had come to buy many copies of our book to go and resell, it dawned on us that the voices we were hearing and the cries were requests to Him or Her that made the women take their lives from Earth. But we wondered if sexual intercourse between husbands and wives was so important that with husbands no more finding their wives desirable just for sex, they would cry for death. It was then that the woman book buyer told us that, "There was no more community between wives and husbands in every area of human life. For you do things in common if there is community."

And as to how she was taking things regarding her husband's loss of interest in her, she said, "In my travels, I am pleasing to the eyes of another man not residing within the coastal city, and I am more with him that a resident of the coastal city. Yet we all cannot relocate. And to which place? Whose city or town? And to be what? And they leaving, or deserting the land of their ancestors, because of one woman by the unwise decision of many men."

"What can we do to help? Kill Godsheren ourselves or get a licensed assassin to take her out?" Dali and I asked.

"Ah! Oh! They that were born near the coast or have lived near the coast cannot be killed. The shedding of her blood will cause raging sea waves to destroy everything and take away the land. And where the sea causes your destruction as human beings, your ancestors cannot receive you into the next world, and you don't have this world or the next world. There then will be no memory of their having lived before."

"I, Swekpee, like all the others, don't wish to die. Our cries for death are not for death but a deliverance from the 'Godsheren predicament'. As for our men, they cannot deliver us, for no person will deliver himself from the desirable and enjoyable. Maybe men from elsewhere could do it if they also don't desire Godsheren and would find her enjoyable, which is definitely the case with our men or husbands," Swekpee explained.

"Oh! We also desired her because of what we heard, but we no more. And we can't speak for other men living on land who have heard about Godsheren," all three of us explained.

"Eh! One woman could take over the whole world because of what men heard about her? She must be a saviour, but we don't know or can't tell. Now that I see it in another light, she must a saviour be to all men till other women are like her," Swekpee explained.

We hosted Swekpee to lunch, after which she left with none of us knowing what to do to help the coastal women because of the new angle that she could be a saviour.

On the night of Swekpee's going away, none of us heard the voices or the cries of the coastal women during the night; but Godsheren's name was still flagged throughout the night.

We discussed the new development.

"She is a saviour," all three of us concluded, and gave no more thought as to what to do next.

But the desire we had for her came back forcefully and we discussed the possibility of hiring an aircraft to go and pick her up, if the coastal men would permit it. But with no aircraft terminal for landing and take-off for aircrafts, we shelved the idea. I, Boo, suggested a helicopter. We agreed because it could land on the school park behind Godsheren's parent's house.

We hired a helicopter that we were later informed by crew, when it was about to land at the designated location as we advised the pilot, made most men and women within hearing range flee because they thought it was about to crash.

Godsheren was brought to Zolita City around midday. And because we couldn't agree as to whom could be 'saved' by her first through sexual intercourse with her, we allowed her to decide that.

Godsheren said, "I preferred the order in which I met you each the first time."

Knowing the order, Dalina and Dabi bowed their foreheads to touch the floor, possibly to acknowledge the 'goddess-liness' of Godsheren like we did Indira and Lindora.

We (she and I) went to my bedroom and she asked me to accompany her to the attached washroom. I did. She washed her face with perfumed soap and rinsed it with water, took off her bra, and used a wet face towel to rub over her breasts, and finally she washed 'down'. She walked ahead of me out of the washroom into the bedroom, and my eyes and thoughts focused on her six-foot frame.

By the side of the bed, she turned to face me and methodically took off my upper clothes and the lower ones. She put her lips to mine, and, with both arms clasped around me, I also doing same, the air-conditioning unit went off. The sudden heat that enveloped the room I couldn't comprehend. It must have been in the 50-degree Celsius mark, because I have travelled to countries that experience such heatwaves and raised temperatures and can rightly guess such temperatures.

She let go of her arms and pushed me away from her, saying, "No, not in this heat. You must be an evil man who the gods want to deny what others have relished. I don't think the other two will be any different. But for purposes of concluding as to whether they are also evil men, I will grant each the opportunity."

She stepped out of my room, banged the door, and a welcome cold wind blew over her and into my room.

She will be right in her conclusion regarding me, I thought. But why the cold wind at the time it did, and when she was going to another man in another bedroom? was the question I asked in my mind.

After four hours, that is before 6:30 in the evening, she came, with Dalina and Dabi in tow, and asked that the pilot fly her back home.

I protested. "Be our guest at a (food) meal?" I suggested.

"I have not eaten your type of meals in many decades," Godsheren answered.

"Then a suggestion: please spend the night in the guestroom. And tomorrow, at the break of dawn, you will be airborne home," I suggested.

"To do what?" she asked.

"We could chat. All four of us in your room," the three of us simultaneously said.

And she reacted loudly saying, "You men are truly evil men because you are married to a god that makes you speak simultaneously the same words. That was the god of the heat (like the sun's) And also the god of light (brightness) like the moon's," she said.

But she agreed to spend the night. And we promised to tell her about our interaction with the sun and with the moon.

"Oh, really? Do you worship the Sun God and the Moon God?" she asked.

"There is no Sun God and there is no Moon God. But there is the sun and there is the moon. We don't worship them. But if you submit to them, and call their names to intervene in any matter that relates to them, namely your living on Earth, and therefore under or below them, they will come in to assist or protect," we, one by one, answered.

"Eh! You imply that you each called on the moon or the sun on the two respective occasions to deny me sexual relations with each of you?" Godsheren asked.

"We each wanted to have sexual relations with you, but the moon on the first occasion, and the sun on the second occasion, prevented it from happening for a purpose," we individually answered her.

"What was that purpose? To starve me of my meals because you had eaten your meals?" Godsheren asked.

"It could be you were eating the wrong meals. And they didn't want us to encourage you to continue eating the wrong meals," we answered her individually, but using the same words.

"That rings a bell. From the night of age fifteen, I left home, met a young man who resembled a snake, actually a python. He gave a gift that I accepted (a diamond necklace) with my hands. He then proposed romantic love to me; but I refused and said, 'You are a python lookalike. You wish to marry me and bring me to your level of looks,' and I laughed mockingly for minutes. He then offered me a fruit and I took it (it was a ripe pawpaw, which

I later learnt meant a romantic love proposal), broke it and ate some. He went his way. And I also went my way.

"A couple of hours later, I fell asleep in my age mate's bedroom and the python lookalike had sexual relations with me. And while he was doing it, I hissed as a snake because of the pleasures. A while later, he climbed on top of me again, and satisfied himself sexually a second time. And I hissed many times this second time, but followed by humming sounds with deep breathing. And since that day, I met him not in human life again. And my life as a result of his sexual acts with me in the dream made me into a new being, eating not the foods that humans ordinarily eat, but what the men give me when they have sex with me."

"It is good we have not eaten as we had planned. You will eat food with us this evening," we individually said to her.

Godsheren lived in our home with us. But when our wives heard of it, they refused to set eyes on her and us. And though we assured them that if what the Godsheren City wives did in the past to their husbands wasn't done by them also, Godsheren would not be an alternate wife ever in substitution to them. But they wouldn't budge. We then told them the Godsheren story as she had told us. And further that Godsheren has no such desire towards their husbands, hence her relating the story and seeking help.

And the admonition from the Godsheren story that we personally learnt is simply: what value your mouth; what value your hands. And the three of us informed our wives.

CHAPTER 6

THE EARS AND THE EYES

Philadelphia, PA, USA
July 29, 2018

Six months into the mysterious disappearance of Godsheren (so some of the coastal people claimed; some also that a big king on the opposite side of the sea separating the coastal city and that kingdom sent armies to capture her for his sole use and enjoyment; a third group claimed she had died), the chief, his counsellors and all men outvoted the women and the city authorities to rename the coastal city officially as 'Godsheren City'. This because if it was true she was dead, it would be in her memory and therefore as a remembrance of her – one woman who touched all men's lives with her sexual acts; and if she was still alive, in honour and as a recognition of her selflessness; and thirdly, if she had been captured by a king's armies for a king's sole pleasure, a reminder that she must be fought for and restored to the city that bears her name.

It was renamed on a Friday night; the time that the city mourned its dead or missing persons or those captured in wars or incursions by tribesmen from far away locations.

When we read the news of the renaming in many countries' newspapers, we hadn't known that the name Godsheren was of many countries interest, and therefore a 'phenomenon' being followed by many journalists.

Dabi, Dalina and I were proud to be associated with her, because one day her secret could fetch us billions of a named currency if we chose to reveal it and she gave her approval, for humans have itching ears for odd or out-of-the-norm news.

Godsheren, when informed by us of all that had been done by the coastal people for her, and the interest shown by many countries' newspapers regarding the 'Godsheren phenomenon' as it was described in many countries' newspapers, said, "The past is history and lives in memories for a time (as long as the youngest person who knew it doesn't die), unless it is written in the heroic annals of the people, though I'm no heroine, but nevertheless outstanding. I hope there is a future for the people to look forward to of one person doing something unlike all others in what he or she would call outstanding and therefore heroic. I hope, too, I will not be that future or part of it for people to look forward to."

When she was done saying what she wanted to say about Godsheren City's future, we felt sad that she wasn't interested in doing something with us that would make us rule the world. For, if the majority of the people of the world are controlled by you in some strange or odd way, the choice of you as a ruler or leader will be yours. But she wasn't interested in being exceptional to all others again. And she is now with us in our home, unknown to others but our wives.

After further six months of Godsheren stay with us, she adopted an attitude of being our sister because we referred to her as 'Sister Godsheren'. And rightly, she no longer covered her body fully and, in the early mornings and evenings, walked in her nighties whether short or long without a morning gown or an evening gown pre-bedtime. And as for her breasts, they were the least of her worries. Maybe because we also wore shorts exposing our thighs and, above all, not covering our chests as we did in the presence of our wives. And who has ever heard of brothers having anything to do with their sister, whether adopted or of the same biological parents? Not heard of. Rare in the world. And especially none at all on our continent. Fortunately, no thought ever arose in our minds of having anything sexual to do with her. And if it should happen, we had had two precedents of the prevention of the intention (we had the intention) in the actual act by Indira and Lindora, the moon and the sun. We felt protected rightly so.

Six long years on, she didn't do anything to show that she was interested in anything sexual with any of us. And that when even our wives had denied us theirs.

Godsheren, in the seventh year, now in her mid-forties, when we travelled with her, saw many couples of elderly wives and elderly husbands (possibly in their late eighties from the wrinkles on their faces) walk into the breakfast area of the hotel we had lodged in hand in hand. She smiled at them, looked us in the face, and said, "Holding hands at that time of life keeps you balanced. But you must start the rehearsal decades earlier. And alone there can't be any rehearsal."

And from that day onwards, Godsheren daily spoke of a rehearsal. When the repetitive nature of it was getting into us, we assured her that brothers are for all times and could be part of any rehearsal with her. We took to laughing at her that she would have a rehearsal with trinity – better than one to one when one dies, as the other is bound to follow minutes later. And so, two days in every week, each of us, before she retired to bed for the night, would take her hand in ours and do a walk rehearsal to her room, chat with her, and when she fell asleep, walk away.

A year went by. Another year commenced. But on the anniversary of that second year (second anniversary of the starting date for each of us), Godsheren said, "The walk rehearsal followed by the two other events are monotonous and too routine, and you each must add to it something different but not by subtraction. If I should decide for each of you, I will add, 'you also falling asleep on the same bed without your body and mine touching'."

We agreed her suggested addition for the challenge it imposed and, after three months of starting, she one morning (of the first day of the two days allotted to each of us), happily announced that she had missed her period. We met on the non-assigned or free day (away from home), and only the three of us, to find who could have been responsible. And each of us protested our innocence of the pregnancy but not the sexual act, and resolved to continue with her till she be delivered of a child through caesarean section because of her age.

We wondered why the moon failed to prevent the sexual act, when even there was not the intention. Moon, knowing the wondering thoughts of our mind (each's mind), sent a letter to each of us with the same explanation that in the sleep state, 'It occurred after the event (in this case the sexual act) was completed, before the realization dawned on the doer, and a completed act the moon and or the sun could not prevent.' Those we prevented were because the intentions were manifested through deliberate acts."

And when the child was born, she looked every two days like each of us and, on the seventh day, like the mother. Then did we remember that while the challenges that led her to hiss as a snake and make humming sounds with deep breathing arose from wrongful use of the mouth and hands (not knowing that they were valuable and must be used with wisdom and discretion), we didn't attach value to what our eyes saw or what our ears heard.

CHAPTER 7

THE SEX OF THE EARTH (LAND)
YOU SHOULDN'T DISBELIEVE

Philadelphia, PA, USA
July 30, 2018

We were walking along the sandy beaches of the Mid-West and not the beach where we had met Indora and Lindora, when Godsheren said, "The sex of the sun is a female, that of the moon is a woman, and that of the Earth, (the beautiful sandy beaches included) is a pretty girl. I mean all three are females, if you are minded to ask me a question on the adjective and the two nouns I have respectively used for each of them."

"Hehehe! Then we must always bow in reverence to the female specie of humanity, for she has been made in the image of the three gods (goddesses), the Earth, moon and sun. We have met Indora and Lindora, beautiful women who merged respectively into the moon and into the sun, proving that the moon and the sun are both females. But the Earth also as a female, we protest," I (Boo), Dabi and Dalina said.

"I have not finished mentioning the other female that will shock you to the core of your bones, and prove to you, your ordinariness. The 'waters' is also a female. And what makes a female are the following: fertility, birthing, nurturing growth, multiplication, pleasure, and speaking and understanding the language of the four goddesses, not gods," Godsheren explained.

"Unless we meet the other two and see their femaleness and they tell us their names, we won't believe you," we, the three men walking with her, said.

"You don't need to see them personally with your eyes and hear their names, but their works will prove to you their femaleness. And if that doesn't help you to believe, two women appearing to you and chatting with you and mentioning their names won't make you believe them as goddesses," Godsheren told us further.

"Oh! Our hearts will be stirred in us that they are goddesses and we would kneel, wherever it is and do obeisance to them to acknowledge there being goddesses," the three said.

"Hahaha! You have knelt before me many times severally, and have done obeisance to me not only after sexual passion but before also. Am I a goddess?" Godsheren asked.

"Oh! You are a female," we answered.

"But that is what I have said about Earth and the waters. Is it they being goddesses that riles you not to believe? Look around you, within the beautiful sandy shore. What do you see? Nests made by sea turtles. They have laid their eggs and they have covered them under the nests or within. Sea turtles that lay eggs are also females. Let us go home, and return after about two months to these sandy beaches at an evening period, and take a look at the nests, and you tell me what you see," Godsheren suggestively said.

And that was how our knowing the Earth and the waters as females and goddesses was shelved for at least two months.

When two months was almost up, Godsheren said, "You men must look up at the moon, converse with it, or let it speak to you as to the timing to go one particular evening to see what has become of the eggs the sea turtles left behind in the nests."

"How could we when we are not females to speak or understand the language of the goddesses?" we, one after the other, asked.

"Oh! But you have met two of the goddesses before, when they chatted with you and blessed you. Whatever language they spoke to you, and you understood and replied, that is the language you should speak to the moon or ask the moon to speak to you," Godsheren said.

"Well, we didn't speak to the moon or spoke with the sun. We spoke with Indira and Lindora, two women or females who blessed us additionally, and who later we saw merge into the moon and the sun respectively," we three answered.

"I won't tell you what to do, as men not being women don't have instant creative abilities, but must be given time to reason out. I will tell you what day's evening we should go," Godsheren mentioned.

Two days later, out in the woods with her and the baby, exactly at eight in the evening, she looked up intently at the moon up in the sky, circularly from west to north, north to east, east to south, and finally south to west, and said, "Tomorrow will be the full moon. And we must arrive on the sandy beaches by nine in the evening. An hour later, you will observe movements from nests into the sea."

The three of us were at the beach early, and she joined later with the baby, we not wanting to miss out on anything that would happen. And as she mentioned to us, a minute after ten in the evening, a first baby turtle moved towards the sea, the waves of which were calm, as if the sea had known that baby turtles would be entering for their first time to inhabit their rightful dwelling. By midnight, many hundreds had followed that first baby turtle in an orderly formation.

"You have seen it with your eyes. We must go home now. The Earth has shown you its evidence that she is a female," Godsheren said.

"There is no need to prove by physical evidence that of the waters or Earth to us. We believe you," each man said, and added, "The four goddesses are females and only assume the form of beautiful women so that when they speak we can understand and act accordingly. But the beautiful women then merge into the four goddesses when their work was done, and therefore kneeling and obeisance must be done to women always."

"Don't disbelieve a woman on a matter related to femaleness of naturally occurring things in the universe," Godsheren advised.

CHAPTER 8

BE CAREFUL

Philadelphia, PA, USA
July 31, 2018

"A woman who is a wife and plays the role of a wife will also play the role of a mother," I, Boo, mentioned to Dabi and Dalina on the third trip outside their country with Godsheren and her daughter.

"Hehehe! Where is that coming from? From her or you? Alternatively, is it a socially known and accepted norm?" the other two asked.

"That is what I have observed with Godsheren. She not only plays the role of a wife, but has been a mother to us in addition to her daughter, no, our daughter. A mother uses the words, 'be careful', a wife not, because they are at par. Also, because she was on Earth before us, (only a figure of speech, implied in this case), and she uses her intuitive knowledge to speak on things that you don't know or have learned. She eats after you or with you, but not before you," I said.

"In what way a mother and mothering roles has she played so far?" the other two asked in a surprise tone.

"Eh! My brothers, her teaching us, her directives on when to go to the beach to observe, guidance and warning to be careful, and ensuring when we return that we are fed, that is nurturing," I explained.

"That is your sole view. But which will you prefer? A wife or a mother?" they asked me.

"Both. I don't wish to make a choice in a case where the two worlds that a woman offers are both excellent and at par," I answered.

"We were hoping that you will opt for a mother so that the wifely duties are rendered to only two," Dalina and Dabi answered.

"Play back or recall my statement. I linked both, and emphasized that a wife who plays her wifely duties will also a mother be. Look around and measure all wives who were or are no more playing their wifely duties . . . they neglect the mother and mothering role of their husbands," I explained.

"Let her mother you on this journey. We have our mothers alive. They will continue to be mothers and play the mothering roles," they answered me.

And while another was about to ask a question, Godsheren (with her daughter Nonan) entered the room where we three were. All three kept quiet.

And Godsheren asked as to whether we weren't hungry. I smiled at the others as they variously answered her that they were hungry.

"Then let's us eat before any other thing," Godsheren said.

Having been done with lunch, and none interested in having a siesta, in answer to her question, Godsheren said, "The questions of one country have their answers in another country. And when you travel find out what answers are in that country for your country, or what questions they have that they can find answers to or for in your country."

"Godsheren, have you travelled to many countries in the past? You don't speak like a philosopher but a realist; like someone who has had practical experiences," the other two but not I asked.

"Oh! Me? How can I? The Earth teaches one thing or another. And there are only two things to learn on Earth. The third is about gods, and goddesses, or the spiritual. And that when you please the goddesses, they expose you to this third knowledge," Godsheren answered.

Incidentally, Dabi and Dalina asked to be excused awhile, to go to the washroom. While there and after it, Dalina whispered to Dabi the words, "Her past experiences with all those men have taught her so much. It is immeasurable knowledge."

"No, it couldn't or wouldn't be. In that act, nobody teaches the other any knowledge. Give her credit for her knowledgeableness," Dabi contradicted him.

And back to where the others were, they boarded the car. And Dalina drove the hired six-wheeler to Buga's, the big market. They bought things by weight, things by measure, and things by volume. And, back at their hotel, they had to store the items with the hotel storage staff and they crossed-checked them. The things by weight, weighed significantly less; those by volume were one third less; and finally the things by measure, were ten per cent less.

"Can we return the things and complain to the sellers about the shortfalls?" the three men asked the storage staff.

"Not in this country and, more especially, the big market. Those who sold to you will have moved from their location to another location," the most senior person with the indicative insignia on his chest pocket answered.

"We ought to be careful on our travels," Godsheren said.

CHAPTER 9

WHEN YOU DON'T RECOUNT SOMEONE'S BAD PAST, YOU WON'T LOSE OUT

Philadelphia, PA, USA
July 31, 2018

It was not many days after our return home from Buga's that Dalina told me and Dali that, when he was in bed with Godsheren, he had had a nightmare and the 'waters' had covered him and were taking him swiftly away and thus he would be drowned, and he screamed loudly and woke her up. (He additionally had not performed his sexual duty as a husband before the nightmare.) After the nightmare, he shook (shivered) like a dry brown leaf, and rushed out to his quarters so that she wouldn't notice his vigorous shaking.

A week later, when it was time for him to spend his two days with her, he fell deeply asleep as soon as he entered her bedroom at a time when she was having her bath. He felt her body touch his, and, instead of romantic feelings towards her, another nightmare of the sun setting him ablaze was his lot. He suddenly woke up and rushed to the bathroom, turned the tap on full blast and drenched himself, having not taken off his pyjamas before entering the bath. He returned to the bedroom unclothed, but Godsheren was deeply asleep, and he felt no closeness or attraction towards her.

It was only at the break of dawn that he fell asleep, but not a sound or well-rested sleep because he was disturbed by the different noises from neighbours' homes and the thought of what happened earlier. He was indifferent towards her during the daylight hours and she therefore asked him whether it was because she slept and he couldn't have access to her that that was why he was indifferent to her. He could, however, not tell her the truth of what happened – the nightmare and after event – and a sudden fear arose in him that he could be pierced with a dagger if he should go near her. The daytime hours ended slowly for him that day.

And another night came. And when he went to lie by her, and stretched one arm to touch her, that arm felt like a wooden boulder with no sensitivity in it and it dropped and hit his face. He therefore restrained himself from any more attempts to touch or do anything romantically to her. When half the night passed, he fell asleep; but again, another nightmare was his lot. The Earth opened its mouth wide like a crocodile to snap him down its throat. And he woke up with cold perspiration due to the fear that he was nearly swallowed and killed.

Dalina therefore decided not to take any more turns when it was his days the following week. But he, not having told the others earlier, took his turn again.

And a fourth time, there was another nightmarish experience. He found himself in the belly of the moon, high up in the sky at the level that the moon is always situated. And, all of a sudden, he realized that he had fallen and was going to crash into a craggy mountain peak. At about three feet before his head would crash into the mountain, he awoke with fright, and he spoke, saying, "No more; nothing to do with this woman."

He didn't return for his second night that week and, when we, the two others, met him, he told us about the nightmares and his failure to perform his sexual duties and other incidents of marriage to Godsheren. He sought to know our opinion on what to do.

"Things have not changed. Times have been normal. Godsheren is still Godsheren. No nightmares but expectancy before and heightened excitement during and after," we answered.

"I am doomed," Dalina said.

"Why? What have you done wrong?" we asked him.

"Nothing that I know off. But the nightmares are battles being fought against me. If it were nightmares involving human beings or trees, I could ask for help from someone more powerful than me to speak to them on my behalf. But nightmares involving the four goddesses, and not four females or women, there is but only one outcome for me . . . my destruction," Dalina expressed.

"Oh, Dalina, you are our brother. Whatever happens to you will affect us also—"

"Hey! Don't say that. You have both said things are better now than before. There is great expectancy and heightened excitement during and after with her. And no nightmares," Dalina interrupted them to say.

"Please, whatever decision you take will affect us," we said.

"It will not affect you adversely. It could only be better for you two not three men to 'share' Godsheren. Instead of two days, three days apiece, when I am out," Dalina said.

"What do you mean by when you are out? Speak plainly," we demanded of him.

"I am withdrawing. I am seeking a divorce from her, but not from you. You can remain as friends, but not brothers. And after it – the divorce – I will travel to a far country and not have any more nightmares," Dalina expressed.

"We are saddened. And let's face it, if the nightmares are being instigated by the four goddesses directly against you, nowhere you go will free you from their action against you," we advised.

"It is the woman. It is Godsheren who is doing it. I know it. I only have the nightmares when with her. Why is it that it doesn't happen on my nights absent from her?" Dalina asked.

"Please, Dalina, when you have problems, don't ask questions. And don't apportion blame on a human being when you are being buffeted or attacked by goddesses. You could offend them more," we advised.

"Who cares if the goddesses are offended the more? Would they increase the frequency of the nightmares then? Then I could only go crazy as a result and eventually die. And, after death, no nightmares could be visited on me," Dalina proudly said as he straightened his shirt and put his chest forward.

"Hmm! A human cannot fight the goddesses, the four of them. They are life, because they sustain life. They could decide to give you a life with nightmares and no craziness and no death," the other two said.

"Like the mark of Cain in the Bible?" Dalina asked them.

"It will be your mark. We don't know how the mark will be made. Whether it will be like Cain's or not, we cannot tell. Maybe you said something amiss or did something amiss. Find out," we advised.

"Whatever, I have said or done, you two will have been accomplices and therefore also guilty," Dalina mentioned.

"Even if we didn't corroborate your statement or act and contradicted you? One lesson we learnt early in life is that from the date you accept anything or anyone, that date is your reference point. You can only look forward and not pre-reference that date or point. And especially with marriage. Whatever happens pre-dating the marriage to you, it is a no-go topic once you consummate the marriage. You have established a new relationship; the prior relationship doesn't matter," we explained.

"Oh! These men would wish to wish away history. What is historical is historical, except it not be known to human beings to be spoken from mouth to mouth or written down for others to read in perpetuity. You mean Godsheren's many thousands of men shouldn't be counted? That is historical," Dalina said.

"Ah! He's said it again. You know that day when you said it in the washroom in relation to her awesome knowledge? I explained that it wasn't true, not that it couldn't be true. It was a no-go matter," I, Boo, spoke for myself this time.

"I will recount her past so that I will lose out. You will not recount her past because you don't want to lose out. The choice should be mine. And the choice should be yours as to what you do with anyone's past. No one should impose his will on another human being," Dalina said.

"One choice. The choice that looks at the past leads to suffering. But the choice that looks at only the future is peaceful and secure," I said.

Dali said nothing in support or against, but rather asked, "If it is continuing act, what must the choice be?"

"I have no answer of my own. But my actions after any continuation would determine what choice the goddesses will spur me to make," I answered.

Then Dalina, at that statement from me, opened the gate to the perimeter fence wall, walked out and said, "I remember, I have a wife. I go to her."

The moon suddenly darkened and every artificial or unnatural light or manufactured light went out and he was heard, saying, "These goddesses are too tough for a man to fight with or withstand. I can't see anything."

CHAPTER 10

THE BEGINNING OF THE END OF LIFE

Philadelphia, PA, USA
August 1, 2018

"When a man no more has a sexual relationship with a woman, from the date he starts implementing his decision, his 'descent' towards sure death begins from that very date," were the words I heard when I stood up to leave the recreational park for home after three hours of looking at the different trees while seated. Who spoke those words? The words were spoken by a woman. Did everybody seated on chairs in that huge park spanning over a mile-square hear the words? What about those who stood still and moved about intermittently? And those walking their dogs, some being guide dogs and other pets? There were many men, women, boys and girls. They were of different ages, doing different things permitted at the park or on the park. None smoked, because it wasn't permitted. None littered, again because it was not permitted. (A man threw a half-bottle of water from where he sat into the waste or trash bin six feet away, but it didn't fall into the bin. He got up, picked it up, and dropped it into the bin.)

They were coming at different times and, after different periods of stay, would go away. There were the birds, cute little birds, numbering as many as the number of people in the park. Unafraid that they would come to any harm, they walked around people, and occasionally perched on the chairs people sat on. Nobody was allowed to feed them but they ate their meals from the green grass.

And as I was recollecting things from the park on my walk home, a mid-sized woman in her late twenties walked past me. I heard a sound and wondered as to where it was coming from because it kept sounding. Then I realized that as her waist shook with each step she took, this melodious inviting sound or song sounded. I was enthralled and decided to keep pace with her by quickening my steps.

Three miles later, she turned right, (while I continued straight on), going away with the melodious sound or song. And later, remembering that most animals make diverse sounds when seeking a partner to mate with, and other sounds during mating and after, I commended her in my heart for putting on her waist beads – singing beads – to attract the right partner to mate with her and during mating produce other musical sounds. I concluded that music or songs and perfumes (through experiences gathered with Godsheren) play an important role in sexual relations among men and women and other living things. And those who sing enjoy their sexual unions best, unlike those who keep quiet so as not to disturb the gods and goddesses who gave such endowments to humans to enjoy, though they also in their own way are females and males.

I got home tired because I had walked a little over seventeen miles that day, and I worked late into the night because Godsheren had been away from home on an assignment for many weeks.

On retiring to bed, I didn't recall thinking or fantasizing about the woman I met earlier in the day for her to appear to me in a dream of night. Yet she sat astride, on my thighs, and it was after four acts with her, (and the healthiness I felt as a result of the release), that it dawned on me that though several men and women were peeping at us, we were not in the least bothered to stop because they were watching and only stopped when we had enough.

We knew that their watching rather than engaging in a similar act would cause ill health in their bodies. And truly, the elderly man among them, of about fifty years, remarked that, "They have left the aroma of the semen around when mine was intact, and I also wanted to have a release. But the women around me will not offer it or if even I plead with them."

I heard him end with the words, "I am dying slowly, but surely as I witness of others fortunate to be engaging in sexual acts, all aspects of it."

My thoughts went back to the park when I was leaving earlier during the previous daylight hours, and what I heard from the female voice and concluded was that women know it all: when to sentence you to death and carry out the sentence they have imposed on you and when not. Then I understood why the woman said what she said and the value of Godsheren.

While away, she permitted the dream so that I would value it for its sustenance of life. Because the day you stop, it is the day your life gradually ebbs away out of this world.

CHAPTER 11

DABI ALSO FALLS BY THE ROADSIDE

Philadelphia, PA, USA
August 2, 2018

Three days after Dalina left and faced unusual darkness and no one knowing of his whereabouts, Dabi also left home without telling anyone, neither Godsheren or I, Boo. He returned on the eighth day after he left, thus being away for seven nights. He offered no explanation for his absence and neither I nor Godsheren asked him to explain the reason for his absence from home. But ten weeks later, on the tenth anniversary of his return, that was a Saturday, he fell ill, and when the Family Care physician came and examined him, the physician diagnosed hypertension. And it was explained to him that it was a life-long disease for which he must take daily medication as there was no cure.

The following Sunday, he suddenly felt unwell again in the morning. The physician was called again, and after various tests and questioning, with a physical examination on the couch in the emergency moving vehicle (the EMV), the physician diagnosed diabetes. Dalina was prescribed drugs again, and informed that it was another life-long disease with no possibility of a cure but could be controlled.

Godsheren and I had hoped that with two diseases suddenly afflicting him, there wouldn't be a third. When Monday arrived, he was doing well with his medications. But by the evening, another call went to the physician. He drove down to our home, asked questions and conducted a physical examination. He ordered laboratory investigations and three hours after the taking or collection of urine, blood and stool samples, the results were sent to him that confirmed the physician's query of leukaemia.

A fourth day came with its symptoms, followed by the physician's attendance on Dalina, and by the day's working hours close, a fourth diagnosis was made of measles. With a newer disease every day, Godsheren told me that by her woman's intuition, Dalina's seven-day absence would be explained by seven diseases being diagnosed.

And so, on the fifth day, the physician phoned our home number just to ask of how Dalina was doing, and Dalina screamed of unbearable pain that wouldn't let go, throbbing and persistent. The physician came over again. He took various scans, because this time he came over in a medical utility vehicle (MUV), which can give instantaneous scans of various body parts. He diagnosed the disease most people don't want to call by its name but by the name 'death sentence': HIV (AIDS). And that was on the fifth day.

Day six was a Thursday. Godsheren asked that the physician should just come to the house around midday. He did. And there was added flu as disease number six. Friday came up with hepatitis. And so was confirmed the intuition by Godsheren.

I had hoped that an eighth diagnosis would not be made. We went through Saturday and Sunday with no new symptoms or complaints.

And being sick, Dalina no more took his turns with Godsheren; the three-day turns every week that Dalina enviously spoke about before he left. But here we were with Dalina not having spent a single of those days with Godsheren. It became my luck or blessing to share her bed to keep her company through chats and the union of man and woman, except for her free day and her off days when she was on her period.

The nights and days and months went by fast for me. But for Dalina, he explained that days were weeks-long and unending, and that weeks were as long as months to him. Because diseases, especially those that inflict pain on you, slow down time; but the joyous pleasures of sexual acts or romance makes time fleeting, reducing days into hours, months into days, and there being no comparison for weeks.

Ten months after the beginning of Dalina's diseases, a woman with a baby girl came to our home, and said, "Dalina is my husband. He fathered this girl. He must come and meet my parents and give the child a name."

"Dalina, you have heard what she said?" I asked Dalina, who nodded but said, "Abena, you know I am not well. Go tell your parents. A man on his sick bed must not give a child a name, so say the sages of the past centuries."

"And so what must I do? Where you cannot give a name for the child, a brother of yours can do that on your behalf. Is this gentleman (referring to me) not your brother?" Abena asked.

"He is a friend. We only call ourselves brothers. He cannot play that role," Dali answered her.

"Then without a name, you won't have anything to do with my daughter. My father will do the appropriate invocation and name the child as his."

She walked out without saying goodbye to us.

I don't know what went through Godsheren's mind when Abena mentioned the child's father. I knew she would not be jealous of a competitor or a rival. But her silence and no body language spoken unsettled me. That day ended.

When we were together, having retired to bed, Godsheren said, "Mark it not in gold letterings but in charcoal writings. Seven children will come out of those seven days absence. I am no prophet, but a woman's intuition works better than prophecy because the prophet could misinterpret the message or hear incorrectly."

With her emphatic statement as to the number of children, my expectation rose of meeting all seven children, but only the time line was uncertain.

The next morning, we had another visitor. A woman with a child on her back came. She asked for Dalina. And she also asked that whatever she had come to speak on, or involve our brother with, we must be present before she spoke.

We three entered Dalina's room. The woman removed the cloth holding the baby on her back and held the child in her hands.

"Amanee, what is your matter?" I, Boo, asked her.

"Please, Dalina slept with me one Sunday night, about nine months ago; no, he had sexual relations with me, and I have since not set eyes on him. He is the father of this child. He called me 'sweetie' throughout that night. But my actual name is Adowa Lynne."

"Dalina, you have 'known Adowa Lynne?" I asked him.

"I had sexual relations with her only one night," Dalina answered.

"One round of sexual relation is sufficient to make a woman pregnant if she was in the ovulation period. And a million rounds may not make her pregnant if she doesn't ovulate, and even then, there have been exceptional cases where a woman who didn't think she was ovulating got pregnant. I hope you don't wish to dispute the pregnancy," I asked.

"I will do the right thing of naming the child. Adowa, please pray for me to heal soonest and I will be not only a father but also a great and darling husband," Dalina said.

Again, Godsheren showed no reaction negatively or positively to Dali's statements. Adowa left and promised to check on Dalina's health status the following week.

Godsheren and I also left him in his room.

A known friend of our family's daughter, Esterina, came on the third day carrying also a baby girl. She asked to meet with Dalina, explaining that since she became pregnant, she only had a text message from Dalina that he was away on duty outside the country. And after that text message, she hadn't heard from him, and she therefore decided to follow-up by a visit to the house to check on his whereabouts.

"Dalina is indoors, but unwell," I told her.

"Is he that unwell? Is it an infectious disease? I am asking because of the child," Esterina asked.

"He can see you both. It might give him hope," I answered her.

This visit, since she didn't ask for our presence, I only tapped on his door, opened it gently and she walked in. Some minutes later, she came out yelling that Dalina pretended not to know her and asked her three times who she was. And when she answered Esterina, he asked, "Is it you, Esther?"

"I won't take a pretence from a man when in the sexual act many times, all night long that day, said, 'As for you, Esterina, I will not ever forget you.' Today he is being forgetful. Maybe he remembers only when he is having sex and soon after. After that, he forgets everything."

"Maybe it is because he is unwell." I sought to explain away Dali's conduct.

"Please, go in with me. Your presence could work a magic, restoring his memory," Esterina pleaded.

And so I went in with her and simply spoke saying, "Dalina, your sweetheart Esterina is here with your baby daughter to visit you. They have missed you!"

"Esterina, I am not too well. I will come over to visit you as soon as I am well," Dalina said.

And she with rage (I saw her facial expression) said, "Did I hear you say to visit? Not to live with us as you promised? If it is to visit, then you might as well die so that not having a man in my life, and therefore a widow, some other man can marry me."

"Esterina, please calm down. It will be alright soon. Let us leave him till another time. Ill health can at times produce the wrong conduct," I advised, and we left Dali's room.

I saw her off to the gate and returned to Godsheren's room, who asked no questions. Anyway, why would she ask questions when she was waiting for the fulfilment of her prophecy; I mean rather intuition.

We did various things the rest of that day and it ended peacefully for us. We slept at night and woke up at the break of another day.

After the morning's hygiene things, I was expectant of two things today (Thursday): the arrival of another baby and his or her mother; and a swinging time with Godsheren at noon before lunch, a tradition we (Godsheren and I) adopted because of the changed situation in our home (Godsheren and us, the three men) and time.

It was a male child and the mother Rosalind who came and met Dalina in our presence, because she requested our presence at her meeting with Dalina, which was some one-and-one-half hour before noon-time

It was near noon-time when she left and we hastened for our time together. We both (Godsheren and I) realized that the more you create from your minds and do, the more heavenly your existence on Earth, with less or no worries to imprison your mind against using them to imagine creative activities or things.

And with cool air blowing in the garden, we took time to stage the beginnings of Adam and Eve in the Garden of Eden, and when breathlessness, not of a respiratory disease, overwhelmed us, we moved indoors for the final cuddling and more, followed by a restful, refreshing and regenerative sleep till supper-time.

Two boys and one girl with their respective mothers, and their mothers' parents came on the next three succeeding days. And it was because the male parents of the mothers said they had a high regard for Godsheren that they (accompanying male parents) didn't set fire to Dalina and create three widows those three days.

At the end of it all, I (Boo) considered thoughtfully what would have happened if the babies and their mothers had all come at the same time on the same day. And since I didn't want to imagine the answer, I went to Dalina's room and asked him as to what was next for him and what he would have done if all the

50

babies and their mothers had come at the same time on the same day.

And in answer to my two questions, he said, "I know I have inconvenienced Godsheren and you. I went in search for variety. I didn't know what made me do it. But none is comparable to Godsheren. But I have lost Godsheren. I will relocate because they will keep coming to cause you nuisance because of what I did. I won't blame them if they are fighting or will fight to have me. Even the gods do that."

Then Dalina stood up with strength that I had not seen with him in months.

"My last moments with Godsheren and you," Dalina said, and walked out of the room in his 'sick clothing' and out through the fenced concrete wall gate as my eyes followed him.

"Hmm!" I said unconsciously.

CHAPTER 12

WHEN YOU WILL NOT BE PART OF
A FUTURE KINGDOM

Philadelphia, PA, USA
August 3, 2018

"Godsheren, Dalina has left us. He walked out of his room and out of the house some fifteen minutes ago," I informed her.

"He is of age. He is not a young adult that will not take an informed decision on what do in any situation," Godsheren answered.

We started as three good friends. And became six when we each married a woman. We had three children each. They are grown up and living their own lives controlled by themselves or directed by the four gods. And along came Godsheren into our three lives, and our three wives left. We became four and lived happily for some years. One left earlier. Another has left. We are now two," I said.

"Why recount history to me at a time like this? A history that I know. Will you also go away? And you are free to do that," Godsheren said.

"I haven't done anything wrong against you and therefore leave you," I explained.

"Maybe, I, Godsheren, have done something wrong against you, Boo, for you to leave me," Godsheren said.

"Oh! No, Godsheren, you haven't done anything wrong against any of us, for us to leave. They did. And therefore left. Those who leave others, leave because they have done something wrong against the person left behind. Wrong attitude and right attitude cannot coexist. But light and darkness coexist with clear boundary lines or demarcation as they fulfil their purposes, none doing anything against the other. Each works within its timelines. The two sexes are like light and darkness. Both equal. Both playing assigned roles. But when one goes to play a non-assigned role, then it feels odd or out of place and departs and will no more play the assigned role. I don't know what to call it," I explained to Godsheren.

"It is called the 'non- kingdomer'. That is what makes you go away. A kingdom cannot be sold or bought. But some give away their kingdoms without knowing.

"I know of a tribal group who are careful about the worth of their kingdom or its priceless nature and have devised tests to value whether the kingdom is about to be lost on a regular basis. And if an attempt is made by someone to take it from them, they are aware and put a stop to it. We will have to travel and visit those tribal people for you to know first-hand what they do to prevent anyone taking away their kingdom," Godsheren explained.

"I would love to go on that trip with you," I said.

"Then first things first, continuing to do things as normally or ordinarily and planning the trip. And the first normal thing is lunch," Godsheren said.

And so, after lunch, we departed our home and for two continuous years, and we stayed in the tribal kingdom. The seasons – the weather seasons – came and went as they were ordinarily to follow each other in the tribal kingdom.

And the last day of the two years, Godsheren said, "The tribal kingdom is a representation of a future kingdom though it lived in the past. Let us move on to see that those two aren't or will not be part of the future kingdom."

CHAPTER 13

WE MESSED UP; AND THEY MESSED UP

Jacksonville, Fl, USA
August 4, 2018

I have wondered many times why Godsheren, since the leaving of us by Dalina also, spoke about various types of kingdoms. First, we had gone to the zoo and followed it up with a visit to a nature reserve the same day, and, at the close of day, and its early evening, Godsheren made mention of the following kingdoms: the animal kingdom, the insects kingdom, the trees kingdom, the fishes kingdom, the human kingdom, and the spirits kingdom. And then she added, "In all these diverse kingdoms, there are different and distinct species comprising each kingdom, except the human kingdom that is composed of only human beings. Whereas in the other kingdoms, there are daily struggles and fights for survival, this ought not to be the case in the human kingdom. But regrettably it is also the case, like in the other kingdoms. And thus the human kingdom is at par with them.

"But some in the human kingdom do not wish to act like in the other kingdoms and even in the human kingdom. They look only ahead. You remember it being said that s/he that looks back is not fit for the Kingdom of God, that is the reason I don't look back and I have not looked back ever. When you look back you find faults and regrets that will sadden you and a saddened person is filled with worries and blinded to the things of the future, and you don't see the hopeful future of a king or queen that you must see. And in not seeing or visualizing it, the past that you know or saw (reality) draws you backwards.

"Dalina has gone backwards. And so also, Dali. Theirs are also kingdoms of sorts. But not of the future. They have messed up. And when the human kingdom messes up, consequences follow. Boo, I invite you to travel with me to the Kingdom of Dalina and the Kingdom of Dali for you to know the consequences first-hand."

We'd stayed in these two contiguous kingdoms, with the same weather patterns under different monarchs, previously, before assumption of kingship by Dalina and Dali. And in the current stay, that lasted six years in all, the first two years presented us with the following weather pattern: the four weather seasons came at monthly intervals. The next two years, the four weather seasons came at weekly intervals, and that was a certainty for the people and the king and they adjusted to it.

Our last two years were unpredictable as to the weather seasons, for we were deceived that the four weather seasons would come daily because the first four days, each took it's turn: winter day one, followed by spring day two. Day three was summer. And autumn as expected came on the fourth day. And then we knew not what. When you were clothed for winter, then there arose the heat of summer, which to some extent was bearable, because you simply took your excess or warm clothing off. But after a further two weeks of that, we couldn't tell, neither anyone or King Dalina or King Dali of the weather pattern. There was no defined time for any of the four weather seasons. All four came at us every moment, so that we didn't want to live life anymore. And after those last two years, when we were returning from our trip to our own land, Godsheren said, "When you messed up, and they also messed up, you are but messed, but they aren't."

CHAPTER 14

TEMPTED BEYOND MEASURE

Jacksonville, FL, USA
August 5, 2018

My office items (writing desks, chairs, computers, fridge, television set, telephones, tea cups and saucers, and whatever makes an office an office) were packed by the roadside one evening without my knowledge.

But strangely, I had a dream the night of the daytime hours that my items were by the roadside, and that my office was at the open space adjoining the road. In the dream, a woman asked me whether there was a watchman engaged by me to watch over the items to ensure that they wouldn't be stolen. I answered her in the negative. By the next morning, all my office items were truly gone, stolen by thieves. I was shocked and despondent.

"I have lost my office and office items or things," I had said loudly to no human, as there was no one with me.

But the woman who spoke with me in the dream of the night appeared in person and hugged me, expressing to me not to worry. "I will take you to places that will make you not only forget the missing items and also the not setting up of an office again. You won't need it. And I am Elenam," she had said.

Then appeared at that instant a ten-year-old girl in our presence. (I don't know how and why I was able to state her age accurately.)

Elenam, seeing her standing between us, said, "This is my daughter. She is ten years of age. Her name Nyuienam, and she will go with us on our journeys to various places but not in the same bedroom with us."

"I am married. I don't wish to marry another woman," I answered her.

"I have not asked you to marry me," she said. And I lost my sense of bearing at that instant. Then she began to fondle me and I protested. And she opened her mouth to say, "Oh! It is because it is an open place. And passers-by could see you and recognize you. As for my daughter, she won't mind. She knows that with a happy couple lies her happiness and ultimate growth with a father figure to ensure her future of a wife and mother when married."

"No, whether it be in the open or an enclosed area from prying eyes, it is still no-go," I answered her.

She moved away from me for a while, while Nyuienam vanished out of my sight. There was darkness all around me. I couldn't see where I was going, though I was walking or moving in a certain direction. I felt whatever I was walking in was compressing my body. I kept moving, but became slower due to the object I was moving through compressing me further. Then I couldn't move anymore. With both arms I felt a concrete-like door or bar against my further movement. My breathing became difficult in the dark, enclosed space I was in. And unable to do anything, I knew death would be next thing. But I didn't want to die and leave Godsheren behind on Earth. My thought went to Godsheren. And I felt a strong desire for her and wished she were around to press her body against mine. Then I felt a body against mine (soft and silky to the touch as Godsheren's) and her hands rubbing along my thighs. I raised my both arms to rub her thighs, and was rubbing when my mind reasoned that it couldn't be Godsheren, for she was no goddess to hear my thoughts and come to fulfil my desire. I stopped reciprocating or echoing what the woman was doing.

"What is that? You have stopped? You desired an enclosed place (all men desire that where they can't be seen and would go through all the processes with a woman) and, with darkness where no human eyes can see you, you have stopped? You aren't going anywhere to another woman. One woman is the same as another woman," Elenam said.

A while later, I felt that I was in another location as the air blowing was fresh; but I noticed that I was falling headlong in a tube-like object. I panicked and my heart nearly ceased.

"Do you wish to go home?" Elenam asked.

"Yes," I answered her.

"Then do what you are supposed to do to me. Once is enough for me, if that will be enough for you after doing it once," Elenam said.

"I think I am dreaming. Are you real?" I asked.

"Take it that you are dreaming and let us have each other. No wife ever beats up the husband or walks out of a promising and eternal relationship because of a dreamt sexual act. You have a defence to put up if ever she should find out. Your mind has helped us for making it known to you that you are dreaming. I wouldn't have thought of that. But a man who admires any other woman and wishes to have a go at her, but is constrained because of a marriage vow, can assume the dream state," Elenam explained.

"But, Elenam, you are real. And I am also a real being, flesh and blood. And I am not in a sleep state and therefore drea . . ."

And without my completing my sentence, I found myself in a room on a bed with her. But my eyes were so much awake that she said, "I will give you a meal, followed by a drink. Alternatively, we could eat from the same plate and drink from the same mug so that you don't think I will make you fall into a deep sleep. You will not be useful to me in that state. It takes two alert parties and participating actively to obtain kindred benefits of a sexual act or acts."

"I understand where you are coming from. But I would rather not eat or drink any fluids," I responded.

"Even food and, say, additionally, water only?" Elenam asked.

"Some foods can do the same thing that medication can do and at times better," I informed Elenam.

"It is because you don't find me trustworthy. If I weren't trustworthy, to keep my mouth forever shut after the act, I would not have asked or implied a sexual relationship with you from the onset. For when you are not trustworthy, you will have doubts about the other party's trustworthiness also. If I have not persuaded you enough, then find your way out," she said, and left me alone in the bedroom.

I didn't not sleep throughout the night; but that day ended and another dawn came, because the birds that only chirp at dawn I heard.

The dark-skinned woman who left me the previous night was not the woman who came at dawn. This woman was fair complexioned, from another race. She sat by me on the bed and was about to give me a peck, when I said, "I haven't done the morning's hygiene."

"Then go and do it. And I will go and prepare you breakfast," she said.

But while I was brushing my teeth, she stood in the doorway till I was done. And she asked, "No bath or showering?"

"Later. Not in your presence," I answered her.

"Even just a sight while you are bathing or showering is not acceptable to you?" She then threw on the floor her morning gown, exposing her body to my stare. And she went on to say, "You know that you are in my house. You have breached my security by entering. And you have breached my privacy by looking at me unclothed. I demand reciprocity, and a refusal will lead to untoward consequences. You could be untrustworthy and tell others about how I look when not dressed. And I will be the butt of mocking eyes and jokes. But he that not only stares at you in admiration, but hugs the body and enters will be a fool to describe it in uncomplimentary language, for then he will also be mocked."

"Which god or goddess do you worship? I can make a vow to that God to keep forever quiet; and breach thereof should be death?" I suggested.

"No, not on your own terms. The breach, thereof, should attract madness. No woman will want a mad husband. But for a dead husband, she will bury, becomes a widow and, two years later, a married woman again without any gossiping about her. Don't you find me attractive?" the woman asked.

"You are attractive. You are no different from Elenam, who brought me to her home," I answered her.

She didn't confirm that she carried the same name as Elenam but came from a different race. And so this woman in leaving me alone in the bathroom said, "You have left me, Marie, in tears. Let it be on your conscience forever."

Another day came and I found myself in a different house. I saw and heard four other women conversing in this house; and because I heard the singing of a fifth woman closer to the room I sat in, I knew there would be at least five women in the house. I was hopeful that they would not all throw darts at me to find out who could 'torpedo' me and drown me in the sea of sexual love, but not the mighty sea (ocean) with rough waves and smooth waves. When the singing stopped, there walked into the room a smallish admirable-looking woman with a yellow skin tone, unlike the second.

She sat opposite where I sat and we chatted for three hours. She didn't ask who I was and why I was in the room I was in. When she was leaving me behind, after the chat, she mentioned her name as Chan and asked that if I needed something I should buzz her. There was no opportunity to buzz her, though I was hungry. And with counting of rafters or roofing beams that I couldn't see, because there were ceilings in place, night fell, and after tossing and turning in bed many times, I feel into a deep sleep for the first time in as many days.

Halfway through the night, I felt a body touch mine, but I was finding the sleep so exhilarating that I ignored the touch. But from 3am, it was as if she was intentionally rolling against me to disturb my sleep for a purpose, because it was happening at five-minute intervals. I woke and out of bed; went to the washroom and brushed my teeth. On my return to the bedroom, I asked her for a mug of hot chocolate drink, knowing that she wouldn't play any tricks but would bring a real hot chocolate drink. She got out of bed, brought me the hot chocolate drink and some cookies. I finished it and asked for additional mug and more cookies.

"Do you want a third mug?" Chan asked when I finished the second mug.

"No, thanks. I need to sit up for a while, for the beverage and cookies to go down well into my abdomen, lest I throw up on you," I said.

"I could rub your back for you to achieve the same purpose speedily," Chan said.

"The sensitivity of your rubs could achieve the wrong purpose," I warned.

"I know how to do it. I will do it like a professional who you haven't paid to trigger anything sensual in you," Chan said.

She gave a couple rubs like a professional. But then I decided otherwise, that I would need a real professional massage, and I would therefore lie on the bed, and did. She massaged my upper limbs and lower limbs and my back. Then I turned for her to work on my abdomen, and a little pressure from both hands on my abdomen sent spluttering into her mouth and face, and she reactively coughed many times. And if she had any thoughts of taming me that dawn period, it came to an abrupt end, for she left for the bathroom and retched many times.

Two hours later, with tears in her eyes, she politely said, "Good morning," and went away.

I felt sad at the turn of events, and noted that with persistence your humanity could be broken down by a number of women. But I had hoped that the woman to break it down completely again should be Godsheren. And therefore, I shouldn't do anything to any other woman to make me feel empathy for her; for empathy for a woman is a spear that the woman can use against you, and no shield can withstand it (an empathy for a woman).

I was distraught the rest of that day because I still could not tell where I was, my bearings, so as to be able to escape if possible.

However, during the early part of that day's evening, I took notice that I was in an aircraft with many passengers, and a woman sat to my left and right, not making any attempt to chat with me. The two women had the looks of the three women I had met already but different colours (races). The woman to my right got up, and for some time I didn't know where she went to in the aircraft for she took too long if it was attendance to nature's call. And at the time she was away, the one to my left pinched my arm many times and bent over and whispered romantic love. She offered that she would be my hostess in one of the first-class suites on board, and pleaded that I shouldn't disappoint her. For she said, "I have not seen a man as glamorous and angelic as you. And when you play hostess to an angel, you will receive godly blessings."

She introduced the empathy card upfront, when I didn't want anything to happen, for empathy to flow to her.

"Please, whether I am an angel or a human being, I ought to be pleasant to you. I am Boo. I wish to know your name because you look like a relative. We could be blood relatives," I informed her.

"I am from the Far East. My father has not travelled before. And, as for my mother, she could not have been responsible for the link you seek to imply. My name Lim Nim," she said.

"What I am implying goes back many generations. It could be at least two centuries, that is five generations," I explained.

"If it is that far removed, then there will be justification to return home with me for restoration of family ties," Lim Nim said and stood up.

I don't know why I followed her. I noticed that as she opened the door to the first-class suite, a strange curiosity arose in me: I desired to know or find out her 'covered' features or areas of the body not exposed to other prying eyes. I therefore made a request to her as follows: "Would you mind my admiring what the 'hidden things', your breasts and navel and . . . hmm . . . look like and more?" I demanded.

"Come closer, so that you can see and also touch to feel," Lim Nim said. It was when her words ended, that there was a sudden descent of the aircraft, and another, and she shouted, "Kikikatsi ja!" ("No, no!")

In panic, I returned to my seat on the aircraft. And when we disembarked, they directed me to where I would be lodging – a small guesthouse, owned by a widow and who would provide me breakfast.

It was in the guesthouse that I practically lost my guard and, on the very night of checking into the guest house, I nearly had sexual relations with the warm and charming Renee. We had eaten a very tasty dinner, a French-type every way, and even late with wines and goat's cheese. We then reclined in rocking chairs, chatting the night away. I felt a little tipsy and, just before midnight, she sat on my lap and asked that I roll her from left to right and right to left just by shaking my body. It was exhilarating. I didn't realize when she pulled the dress from under her buttocks, and stretched her right hand out and gradually unzipped my pair of trousers to take out my genitalia, that was coincidentally erect, that I remembered that I was there not on my own volition but by compulsion. I restrained that hand and kissed it passionately, assuring her that the future gives more than one midnight of twosome-ness.

Later, the next day, my traveling companions came over and we set off on a train ride all day long, arriving at the couple's home that I was to stay at the stroke of 6pm local time. The couple hosted me for dinner and afterwards showed me my bedroom for the night. I had a warm shower. And went to say goodnight to them in the living-room. They responded in the same manner. But the wife, so I thought, rose from the armchair and followed me to my doorway, said, "A goodnight kiss, my love." She planted three kisses on my lips, and I felt the wetness of her saliva on my lips and licked it unconsciously.

"Oh! Dear, I didn't ask to know of your name," I said.

"It is customary for a woman not to give her name to a man whom she has met for the first time and whom he has not known, the Biblical knowing implied," she answered.

But then she suddenly collapsed and was frothing from the mouth. Having earlier read that a person's name was important to call the emergency services in their country, I lifted her skirt a little and saw the name 'Hongho' written on her thigh. I made the call and the first responders arrived in five minutes, by which time she had stopped frothing and was breathing normally.

When I realized that I had not fallen to the sexual snare of Hongho also, then it dawned on me that there would be at least three others after her to put me through a test of sexual fidelity to Godsheren. For I recalled that some years past, Godsheren had mentioned to the three of us men, who were then friends and newly married to her that, "If you find a particular beautiful and attractive woman among one colour of people, there are seven others like her or who resemble her but have other skin colours, making a total of eight different colours but all look alike in features."

My next test was on another continent. Lim Nim and her friend accompanied me again. We arrived at a time when the locals were celebrating the nighthawk festival. The women dress like hawks at sunset and mount high-rise buildings and jump from the top of the buildings. And it is the responsibility of a man to catch her while on the descent so that she won't come to harm.

Lim Nim and her friend decided to be part of the festival. Lim Nim chose a local man to catch her during the jump, and therefore the descent, so that she wouldn't come to harm. Her friend chose me and in doing that mentioned her name as Aika. Aika did three jumps at sunset that day, and I had to catch her before she fell to the ground and came to harm or got injured; and each time I did, she held me firmly, supposedly out of fear, but gave hugs to arouse sexual feelings in the 'catcher' – me. Truth be told, I was aroused; but when we went back to our lodging, I pretended to be unwell and she only looked at me till I fell asleep, and she didn't disturb me throughout the night because, in her race, they don't use force to procure sexual relations but cunningness.

When we arrived on another continent, the two women, Aika and Lim Nim, took leave of me after handing me to Natalya.

She played the organ for me many hours. In the evening, she played the flute as she sat by me on the bed. And as she played, my sense of bearing was gradually being restored, but not fully.

I woke up the next day with her staring at me. She, however, said, "You have missed Natalya's love that only comes from Lushia. I will not have any memory of you. And you will not have any memory of me."

My sense of bearing now fully restored, I travelled alone on a train that broke down just a thousand kilometres from my home. A lady traveller in the next compartment, when we disembarked, offered for us to rent a room with two single beds for the night, she explaining she was low on funds. I took her offer as I didn't have enough either. In the night, she said, "You don't know me from Adam. But you were good to me. I wish to have you in my memory, unforgettable memory, not on and off. We could share a bed together. And the hotelier the next day, finding one bed unused, will not bill for two single beds but one."

"I would love to do that, but I coughed a while ago and you heard it. I would not want to mar the memory you would have carried away," I said.

The next morning I was back home and, some hours later, Godsheren also returned from her trip.

"Hope you were not tempted beyond measure during my trip?" Godsheren asked.

"Hmm! It was beyond measure!" I answered.

CHAPTER 15

A LIFE OF TWO ONWARDS

Jacksonville, FL, USA
August 6, 2018

Our day, every morning, began at 5:00am. Ten minutes was hygiene time; after which we read the Holy Bible with the singing of songs of praise and adoration for the next thirty minutes.

One hour in total, with thirty minutes in the orchard at the back part of the house talking to the fruit trees, namely pear, orange, mango, lemon, pawpaw and coconut trees. We saluted them as we did among ourselves. We forgot not any day to thank and praise them with words of greetings. We had conversational time with the plantain and banana plants also in our time in the orchard rituals. The hours between 6:20am and 7:00am in the mornings were spent inhaling the freshness and sweet-smelling flowers in our front triangular garden, admiring them, offering thanks and praise to them for their goodness to us, additionally watering them or removing weeds.

We didn't fail to observe a night-time prayer of one hour between midnight and 4:00am of the next day, individually and independent of the other.

It was such a healthy and warm relationship with the flower garden and the orchard that we counted the many years passed that we used hired labour for the works in the orchard and flower garden, an irreversible loss. And we daily made mention of the four goddess's roles in both gardens. We thought rightly that no couple who did the daily morning rituals would ever divorce each other.

Don't think that we didn't at dusk walk through the two gardens again, but at a quicker pace, telling them of our best wishes for the night.

The times were and are stressful but the rewards were and are not measurable, with no ill health visits to the family physician but only the six-months regular medical check-ups. There were days, however, we both missed or one or the other didn't take part in everything on the daily planner.

Our breakfast time was and is enriching as any of us prepared breakfast, laid the table, but we always ate together. And depending on what else we would be doing that day, we had a quick shower together or separately.

We have not had such bonding when we were four, three good friends (men) married to one woman, compared to the new state of a man and a woman. Then, (the past of three men and one woman), we were not only disparate individuals but disunited.

With such bonding, because we did everything together, even the mere thought of doing something in one person's mind reflected in the other's mind, and we were achieving success of one kind or the other. We were especially glad that it was at a time, the 'empty nest' time, when proactively most couples live their lives independently of each other and therefore firmly on the divorce road to divorce that good fortune of bonding smiled on us (Godsheren and I).

A year on of the 'two in one' only, and on a wintry evening, Godsheren asked, "Boo-lem-Boo, (Boo, tie me with a rope or twine), did you ever read of any couple who ever lived on Earth and did everything exactly the way we have done and will do twenty-four hours of each day and as bonded as we have been blessed with? We are the first. And we will leave our examples behind for others to follow."

"Hahaha! Godsheren you have answered your own question. But my answer: no couple, married couple, of a woman and man with an empty nest, when it was the full nest that held them together, has lived as we did and are doing. It is not recorded in any books of humans. And even the gods have not revealed any such. Though when you asked the question I asked for a revelation of any such couple. Our bonding is like the bonding of the four goddesses: the sun, the moon, the waters, and the Earth. They are wedged together. And we are wedged as they are," I answered.

"Then there is no end in sight for us. I mean, there will be no death for any of us; as much as there is no death for the sun, moon, waters and the Earth," Godsheren said.

"Ah! Oh! Eternity arises through bonding, from that walk in the two gardens conversing with naturally endowed things of the four goddesses and doing other things together and sealing it with life-regenerating sexual love at night," I mentioned.

"Hehehe! It is not only at night since the start of the fourth month. And it is not limited to the bedroom. Both gardens have even looked on us in admiration and listened to the endearments we showered on each other as we did to them also. And they have blessed us with blowing cool fresh air at such times, and a sweet-smelling aroma around us and on us," Godsheren stated.

"It must be a life of two onwards and doing the same things every day but, each day being different, different things," I said.

And Godsheren said, "With practical demonstration," and she kissed me in the orchard as I leaned against the coconut tree and reciprocated her kisses and added others.

CHAPTER 16

GODSHEREN CITY MOURNS GODSHEREN'S PARENTS

Jacksonville, FL, USA
August 7, 2018

"I must go and mourn my parents," Godsheren said one morning after our time in the two gardens.

"Wuiwui! Are they dead? How did you get to know? And I don't know?" I asked her.

"They aren't dead. But I have a premonition that within two days they will die, one after the other, with my mum going first and my dad after her," Godsheren said.

"We can pray against their dying. We can do something. We can airlift the best doctors to go and prevent their deaths," I countered her.

"It will take three days of continuous flying time to get to them, even that by military jets that fly at 1,500 miles per hour. And only two countries in the world boast of ten of such aircraft, five apiece. And I am not of the status that can commandeer such aircraft. Some die because of lack of status. And others die because of lack of funds by themselves or their child. And I belong to both groups.

"It is fifty years since I left them. My parents as I knew them aren't afraid to die, to live the next existence. They both spoke of the next life that they would begin forty days after death on Earth, and would not need food to be put in a bowl outside the gates of the house to eat those forty days while awaiting the special water vehicle that would ferry them; for all dead must travel on water to a new life within water, not on land.

"It is only murderers and liars on land when they are dead that need family members to put food in a bowl outside the gates of the house that they lived in for them to eat those forty days while awaiting the special purpose water vehicle.

"I'm not fearful of their death, but just the sorrows and tears that follow because I'd see them not again with the human eyes or hear their voices or feel their touch as I snuggled against them. Three of the human senses gone and you being deprived of those, their three senses," Godsheren explained.

"Then, when it happens, we must go and mourn them," I suggested.

"We don't have a choice in the matter of mourning. However, apart from deferring and not being at the burial because of ill health, we must of necessity go and look at their clipped or cut fingernails, toenails, plus the hairs on their head, shaven and kept in an urn or matchbox and, thereafter, on the eighth day of death, buried before their ascent (it is described or called 'luvor') on the fortieth day for the next life in the waters," Godsheren said further.

We lived the next two days (before her parent's death) with expectancy, and did everything as normally as possible; but only that Godsheren started wearing scarves on her head to cover her hair completely – a symbol of mourning. I also shaved off the hair on my head completely in preparation for the act of mourning.

"News flash: Godsheren City in mourning," the newsreader announced.

Godsheren knew it would be about her parents and so she got up from the chair and went to one of the many bedrooms, leaving me behind to hear the full news item. Here are the details of the first news item:

'The parents of Godsheren, after whom the Godsheren City is named, are dead. They died one hour apart of each other. Their family members are in consultation with city authorities and will announce dates and other arrangements for their burial rites and burial in due course. The Godsheren City mourns unsung parents.'

With tears in my eyes and my nose dripping I went through four bedrooms and found her in the fifth.

"Godsheren." I held her in my arms. "I love you. Your parents lived well on Earth, though not millionaires. We will also live well on Earth and make others millionaires in their memory. I will arrange for flights. We must set out tomorrow with the first departing flight," I expressed.

"Please, ensure to get a caretaker for the gardens. That should be for a period of forty-four days away, plus ten traveling days," Godsheren advised.

I didn't know that in times of bereavement, and therefore in mourning, love can be so strong that you still feel passion for each other, and keep hugging each time your paths cross in between duties to be performed for the dead or to others, and because you feel sympathetic and empathetic in both directions, because you are both bereaved.

Her tears dried by flight time next morning. And throughout the trips, that is, connecting flights and transit times, Godsheren recounted various events about both parents. *Ah! I wish I had recorded them*, I had said in mind. *But, when mourning, it is best to listen to your spouse with attentive ears and focused looks at her, than be distracted by things that will not increase your love investment in her*, I said again in my mind.

Stressed and tired we arrived after fifty years of her being away from Godsheren City. And because it was night time, not many people saw and recognized Godsheren.

It was only one customs and preventive officer that I heard say, "That woman looks like Godsheren," to a younger colleague.

And the younger man in turn, asked, "Ah! So she gave her name to the city?"

"No, it was named after her," the elderly officer said.

Godsheren recognized her surroundings and therefore home easily, especially as the number of coconut trees behind the house (though possibly replanted) remained nine. I would ask her Why nine? but at a suitable time or not at all.

I was so, so refreshed by the morning. For Godsheren had said, "In mourning your loss, the wise don't create another loss." And she did something practical that night that created that state and gave her also a glow.

Hmm! Maybe her people, the Godsheren City people, don't die young but till they are one and half centuries of age, I had said in my mind when the chief (in my presence, described as a king) and his counsellors and the city's mayor came to console the bereaved families and saw Godsheren and they were introduced.

The mourning atmosphere changed within fifteen minutes of their arrival as the king summoned the 'Kinka' (celebratory group) dance troupe to come and beat drums, sing and dance for he said, "Our daughter and wife was dead or lost or kidnapped, but she is alive, found or restored."

After two hours of beating of drums, singing songs and dancing, Godsheren danced with the king, and later with me. The king then said, "Godsheren City will only mourn Godsheren's parents and not Godsheren. For Godsheren is the soul and spirit of Godsheren City. Through her, the life expectancy of the city has increased. And there is no ill health or chronic diseases to take my people's lives until they say it is enough by themselves, and to a life within the waters, I or we go. And as her parents have done."

"Eh! Without asking Godsheren my question as to the Godsheren City people's long lifespans, the king has given me an answer," I self-spoke.

On the fifth day from the date of our arrival at 3:00pm, Godsheren's parents were buried side by side in one grave. In life, they were one couple and, in death, one couple. And the hope therefore is that in the next life under the waters, if they do marry, then they will be a married couple there also. But if not, they will be friends.

The king and all his counsellors were at the cemetery with Godsheren and me.

Godsheren laid the first wreath, and was followed by the king who also laid a wreath. When it came to the turn of the mayor, he cried so loudly that many others also started crying and, in turn, Godsheren and I. That set us back thirty minutes as to the funeral program's timing. But who are we to complain about time when the emotions of some are triggered, and time is wasted, but humans must hasten other events on the program drawn so as not to stress those who are involuntarily stressed by time, thus the 'time stressed ill health' in the medical lexicon.

The late lunch after the funeral as it went on was interspersed with drumming, singing and dancing. There were four groups, three traditional drumming, singing and dance groups, and one Christian religious group. Incidentally, this group also drummed, sang songs and danced a dance with known names unlike the Agbadza, Atsiagbekor and the Kinka dance groups. It was like whichever you enjoyed dancing or watching, go dance or watch. We closed at 7:00pm and Godsheren provided takeaway packs to everyone because the funeral lunch was by courtesy of the king and the mayor.

It was fourteen hours that Godsheren was on her feet that burial day. After supper, I asked her to put her feet in a warm bowl of water that I boiled and brought to her. I massaged her lower limbs, not with the intention of any type of reward. Additionally, I asked her to partially undress for a whole-body massage on a compressed into hand luggage size (of twenty inches by seventy-two inches by six inches thickness) expandable massage bed that gives off whiffs of invigorating aromas.

"What an awesome surprise, dearie," Godsheren said after one hour of body massage.

"When a man and a woman live for each other, (not in competition to be recognized and given awards), they develop proactive minds that provide answers to future events," I mentioned.

"What next must we do?" she asked.

"A bath or shower and then retire to bed and Godsheren sharing a story of her childhood as a bedtime story," I answered.

73

"There could be other things in addition to the bedtime stories from the past. But, as they are of the future, it is best to let it be a surprise," Godsheren said and took off the rest of the clothing –the underwear on her.

The next morning after breakfast, with four other family members, two from the mother's side and the other two from the father's side, we drove to the king's palace to thank him and his counsellors; then a drive to the mayor's to do likewise. We later fellowshipped at the local community church and expressed our thanks for their role.

By 2:00pm, we were back home. And thought of how best and where to meet the three traditional dance groups to express our appreciation. But all three groups entered our house compound with different types and sizes of drums, congas and other instruments, set up in their various groups, and drummed, sang and danced till the break of evening.

Some women relatives, cousins and nieces of Godsheren present in the house, served them various types of choice food and drinks. And after, Godsheren raised a song, "Akpe, akpe . . ." (This could mean 'thanks'; but could also mean 'a thousand' if used in association with a number, and therefore implies that number of thanks.) And Godsheren added the words, "Manya gblor," or indescribable thanks or gratitude.

On the eighth day from the burial day, certain traditional rites, including the burial of 'luvor' occurred, with hair removed from their heads and nails cut from their fingers and toes being buried in the house; the essence of that being that the dead are no more among the living and therefore will not see their hairs growing in length or the nails also growing in length, the only two things that living humans can see the growth of, but not any other feature of the human body is seen growing in length.

We returned to the normal everyday things of life from the ninth day onwards, and it was not until the fortieth day that the ceremony of the dead departing land to travel by boat (a special purpose vehicle) to live in the waters was performed at dawn.

And with our departure from Godsheren City in a few days' time, we went to tell the king and counsellors and to bid them well and they wishing us a safe passage.

"You will be a queen one day," the king mentioned. And realizing it could be misunderstood, added, "You will be king in your own right, not a queen through marriage. But you will be called a queen because of your gender, and because the world desires to have the distinctions as to one sex or the other, hence my mentioning the word, 'queen'."

"But I am not from the royal family?" Godsheren answered.

"Well, the people of Godsheren City and other people will enthrone you. We will meet you some days before the first anniversary memorial celebration," King Giteza said.

We visited the mayor and few others, including friends and family members, to inform them of our departure.

CHAPTER 17

THINKING AHEAD

Jacksonville, FL, USA
August 8, 2018

The third morning of our return from the two funerals, Godsheren indicted that she would fast that day, and said, "The royal families in every kingdom groom their successors to take over the throne from the occupant when he or she dies or through abdication. But not ever has a non-royal been groomed because a non-royal (not by birth), in the palace or royal courts, will a murder commit on royals by birth to inherit the throne."

"But the king knew you are not a royal by birth but spoke up of you becoming a king (queen) and therefore at a later date would invite you to the palace to be groomed," I said to her.

"When other prospective royals haven't spoken that they aren't interested in being enthroned as king or queen?

"Maybe a spirit or a god spoke to the king to say what he said, but royal family members are averse to obey spirits or gods in the matter of succession to the throne, as that amounts to usurpation of the throne by spirits or gods through their adherents. Moreover, royals are trained from birth not when they are in their sixties. I will groom myself, for if even I am invited to the palace to be groomed, I will go as an identified 'usurper' and I *will* be killed, not could be killed.

"But if I were to go, where would you go or be? For the king said nothing about your future. And moreover, royals and non-royals don't compete against each other in any game or sport. Not even the sport of romance openly and publicly. It will be done in secrecy," Godsheren explained.

"It is tricky, then, when one royal speaks, but other royals don't countermand what is said or protest against it. Ah! You don't get it. The countermand or protest none will be able to do, for as long as the king or queen, who decreed or spoke about the succession, lives. For his or her word is law within the court of the palace, and all must be obedient to the edict unless the chosen successor be sooner dead than the king or queen who chose him or her," Godsheren said.

"Then treachery will work in king's or queen's palaces as both a sword and a shield, depending on who spoke or who didn't speak," I mentioned to Godsheren.

"What the king said was from the four goddesses, and treachery has formed in the hearts of the other royals against me. But what the king can't do, the four goddesses will do. But I must not be within the palace with the other royals or the counsellors," Godsheren explained.

"What does the grooming entail? I have not lived in a king or queen's palace or court in the past to know. But from the meaning of the word, someone who knows about palace norms and etiquette must train you," I said.

"You are right. But the goddesses know all the norms and etiquettes and will teach by revelation, or even take human or angelic form to teach, and that is even better because your failure as king or queen would be blamed on them, not on a human groomer from the palace," Godsheren said and added, "The human groomers are incidentally commoners who have worked in palaces for many decades, and have become authorities on norms and etiquettes and pass on their learnt knowledge and etiquettes but not wisdom.

"Wisdom is endowed by spirits and goddesses. And a king or queen who didn't have the favour and support of spirits or the goddesses won't have it. That is the reason why King Solomon of the Bible was highly regarded for his wisdom, but no other king or queen in history. And the Queen of Sheba attested to that. I will ask for wisdom to rule and I have already started from the first day of our return from the first trip, the saving of the city and all its people from total destruction," Godsheren mentioned.

"Then will you share some of the divinely endowed wisdoms you have received? King Solomon's wisdom was more on judging rightly between parties. Yours would involve judging, economic policies, energy matters, health and wellbeing, sanitation policies and security," I, Boo, mentioned.

"That is wide-ranging. But whatever you ask, seek or knock on the doors of the four goddesses, they will grant you. After dinner, I will start telling you wise words regarding the kingdom's economy," Godsheren said, and pushed prospective kingdom-related issues till the evening.

She broke her fast minutes before 6:00pm.

I didn't have to remind Godsheren on the subject she promised to talk about, but with suddenness she started telling, and even that by telling of a vision she had two days' earlier.

"In my vision of the night, I saw male quintuplets who had attained majority or adulthood. And any time they wanted or felt for sex, they would attack and beat up their elder sister, who was two years older than them, and one by one take turns to have sex with her.

"The vision shocked me and, for the rest of the night, I couldn't sleep. And my thoughts for half of the daytime hours were on the essence of the vision, and why and what its importance was or is. Then I heard the voice of an elderly woman, but it sounded like my mother's voice, and since my mother is buried some two months earlier, it implied that an ancestress (being dead, she has become an ancestress) wishes to explain a matter that will have future implications for me later in a garden.

"And that was why I stopped in my stride – you remember I told you before sunset, while we were in the garden, to be quiet for a while till I said otherwise, and gave you no reason and was glad you didn't, like some men or women, ask for a reason for any request or demand made on them or to them, before complying with the request or demand – and this was what the voice said:

'The quintuplets refer to a future kingdom that will begin and within two years grow five times in size and, again, the quintuplets mean that the kingdom will be five times more powerful than other kingdoms. Further, the quintuplets also mean that within five years of becoming a monarch, the burdens inflicted on the kingdom will have to be completely removed. And that means each year of those five years you must reduce the burden by one-fifth and therefore complete the removal in five years.'

"'The elder sister you saw in the vision, who they beat up and had sexual relations with any time they desired sex, refers to all humanity in the kingdom and who are carrying burdens difficult to carry, and which must be done away by a monarch that will come on the throne. And also, that their sister had water that the quintuplets desired, because it is the only water that quenches thirsts. And because the water comes from within her, so the water for humanity in the kingdom must come from the bowels of the Earth,' and the voice ceased."

"I don't understand what the voice told you. It means nothing. It makes no sense. I hope it does to you," I replied to what Godsheren said.

"You have seen the surface water sources that the Godsheren City use for every household activity and industries. And you have seen the four electricity poles with light bulbs in the four corners of our house that come on at evenings or whenever the sky turns dark or black. The poles are mounted on water boreholes (drilled in rocks) and each pole is safely secured with six metal clips or struts, and which water is our source of water because the water from the bowels of the Earth are clean and healthy and taste great, unlike water from surface sources.

"The new source (underground or from rocks) of water must be replicated in the kingdom for the people or subjects of the queen to use. And not only that, in providing water at each electricity pole-mounted location, you also light the community with lights to keep darkness away.

"But that is not all the explanation for the vision. The burden imposed on the woman (their sister in the vision), that is beating

79

her up before having sex with her, refers to taxation on the people or subjects, that was exacted at regular intervals. Yet the king would want to receive the pleasure of the subjects as the woman (the sister in the vision) gave the quintuplets pleasure, but she not having like pleasure. And the five-year period is the time limit to abolish every form of taxation on the subjects, which incidentally will be removed gradually over the five years, and no taxation will exist in the kingdom. The queen will only sell water and light to the people to maintain the kingdom and to build the infrastructure of the kingdom for its welfare, defence and security," Godsheren said.

"That will be the only kingdom on Earth to abolish every form of taxation. But how will you finance the building of infrastructures, like the water systems with the mounted electricity poles with bulbs to give light?" I asked.

"I have a diamond-cut (hexagonal pearl) 'Kesinonu' that will finance the construction of infrastructure and installation of water and electrical systems, as I mentioned earlier, at every fifty-foot interval across the kingdom. It was an inheritance from my parents. When you cut and sell a part of it, it grows back to its original size and shape. When my parents noticed that, they said they would live a simple life in this life (on Earth), and when they were buried like royalty on their death, then and only then would I inherit the diamond hexagonal bar, and also inherit a kingdom alongside and use that resource to establish five times the size of the inherited kingdom.

"It will be unlike other kingdoms that ever existed, because their royal families built their kingdoms from the resources of the people (subjects), but a true king or queen must build the kingdom from his or her own resources. And so far, only Mawu (deity), who is also known as the Nya (word) has tried to build nations and kingdoms through some people by giving those people resources, but the leaders kept the provided resources to and for the leaders.

"And this is the first step I will take. I will build the new water and electricity systems – the queen's water and the queen's electricity systems – in Godsheren City, one hundred feet apart initially (later to insert a water and electricity system at the fifty-foot intervals within six months of my coronation as queen), and complete them before the first anniversary of my parent's death–"

I interrupted her to say, "You have only a little over eight months to do all that. Are you able?"

"I am more than able. I will engage one thousand firms for the task. Each will just take four months to complete the required quantity in its assigned counties and suburbs," Godsheren said.

"I hope the benefit we have had of two gardens, a flower garden in front of dwelling houses, and an orchard at the back of the house, will be available to your subjects also?" I asked.

"By the time the fifth kingdom is added to make one big kingdom, 'the Godsheren Kingdom', I will have reconstructed all dwelling houses with two gardens and a multipurpose sewage system. The Queen's Habitats, they will be called. And, a year on, the fifth added part will have theirs," Godsheren explained.

"Wow! And how about the construction of private business buildings?" I asked.

"They will be built by the business owners through their own finances or resources, but in accordance with approved queen's layout and specifications and connected to the queen's water, electricity and multipurpose sewage system. The subjects must work just like the queen to earn a living to buy water and light (electricity). And those who cannot set up businesses themselves, or get employment with those who will set up, will work in the queen's various services and be paid to be able to buy water and pay for light," Godsheren said in answer to my question.

"Hmm! Yours will really be the true kingdom. Those who have had kingdoms in the past ages weren't true kingdoms from what you intend doing in your kingdom. I am glad to be part of that kingdom, and to experience the differences between yours and theirs (which can only be found in historical records). Please, Godsheren, I look forward to hearing more another day. I will take my turn to prepare today's snack," I said.

"I will be with you in the kitchen, queen or not, for queens also eat and queens must prepare the tastiest foods, because they must have super brains, super intellects – something distinct and different from their subjects," Godsheren said.

CHAPTER 18

THE SEA BROKE DOWN ITS OWN TEN CENTURIES' SET BOUNDARIES

Jacksonville, FL, USA
August 10, 2018

I had slept beyond the usual waking-up time to rise and walk through the gardens and converse with the fruit trees and flowers that Monday. And Godsheren didn't wake me up either. And it was not until an hour after the rising time that she violently shook me and woke me up, saying, "All the seas have broken their own set boundaries and coastal towns or cities are being submerged under swift-flowing seawaters. Rise up. Get ready. We must save the Godsheren City and people if they are not dead by now. No, I will go ahead, follow after."

The next thing, I heard the words, 'Zapata loo' spoken by her, and she vanished out of sight. I didn't brush my teeth but peeled a banana and ate, put on my clothes, uttered the words, 'Zapata loo' twice, and was airborne and travelled through the clouds. I caught up with her just before her descent upon land. I had flown at twice the speed she flew at, hence catching up with her. We saw the raging swift-flowing seawater carrying boats and ships against each other and destroying them, and the planks of boats and scattered ruins of ships hitting the coastline viciously, and therefore we landed five hundred feet away from the coastline, so as not to come to harm. And, as we were heading towards the seashore, we saw people of various ages running inwards (opposite us) in various states of clothing or unclothed.

We turned and followed them for a few seconds; but when we saw that the waves had covered some houses and drowned some, we ran in a direction perpendicular to the swift-flowing seawater, and I drew a line in the sand, and Godsheren following, carrying a 50ml bottle of perfume, sprayed it intermittently on the line I was drawing in the sand. And the waters stopped at the line in the sand, and that way a two hundred-mile stretch of coastline had new boundary marks or lines and the waves subsided, acting serenely as if a few minutes earlier on, it was not boisterously swift-flowing causing devastation.

"We must count the cost of destruction," Godsheren said to me.

And for the next many hours, as we moved by means of the wind carried two feet above the sand, we saw corpses in the thousands of grandfathers, grandmothers, fathers, mothers, sons and daughters of various ages, fishing nets, ruins of houses and ships.

At the end of the counting of the cost, Godsheren said, "Nature must bury the corpses and everything so that no other living will see but conclude that some have been taken away mysteriously with their properties."

And with that statement, she knelt on the sand, I also did, and she scooped the sand in both hands, again I also did, and spread the sand in each hand in two cardinal point directions, and I echoed what she did. We then went home, her parents carried by the wind again.

And at home, she explained as follows: "No living must see with eyes what we have asked nature to do. They must only see the result afterwards."

Not a soul was at home. No animals either, those kept in homes. And all was so quiet that we heard our breathing as sounds. I felt some uneasiness and she, noticing, said, "No human being can run any race faster than water and, therefore, when you are ten miles away and you hear that water or seas have begun running, flee by means of the wind, as the wind that carried us."

Is this woman a goddess? I would have asked, but didn't.

And at sunset, and followed by the full moon giving us light to see the wonders of nature, we returned to the new seashore and I saw a stretch of beautiful, clean sandy beach, but without coconut trees that were there previously.

She must be a goddess, I said in my head without equivocation this time.

Three days later, the people started returning to their homes, for we heard voices and sounds. By one week later, most activities had returned to normal, and when Godsheren and I heard that they were going to make count as to what the sea had taken away in its anger because some people had offended anyone or more of the four goddesses, we knew our time was up. We must return home, for Godsheren had mentioned to me some days earlier that, and I am quoting her words: 'When you act on behalf of any of the four goddesses to save a situation, you must not take credit for it. If you do, you make yourself equal to a goddess. And next time, they will punish you along with any other person they wish to exact a punishment on.'

We left in the manner and mode we came. And when we read newspapers or listened to news bulletins of some countries, the stories were about the outright destruction of all their coastal towns and cities. But the saving of Godsheren City will not have an explanation and be a mystery that they (newspaper reporters) will not be able to explain till another century, unless Godsheren and I tell them what we did that troubling day.

CHAPTER 19

THE FUTURE QUEEN'S SHEPHERD VISAS
AND BECOMING A SUBJECT

Jacksonville, FL, USA
August 10, 2018

I, Boo, told Godsheren of a dream I had and, a few days later, that I had the benefit of in real life. In my dream, a seven-year-old girl was in front of a palatial building and men came in and went out. I was about to enter the same building when she undressed and laid on her back and she asked that I shouldn't only look at her with shock and surprise but to do it. Because she needs the money for her aged parents and her own use. And she emphasized that some coloured persons who visited Godsheren City from their home countries from time to time loved it with her. I felt revolted.

But I was surprised that a few feet away from where she lay were many bundles of a green type of currency which, if she saw and took home or handed it over to the rightful owner, she could be rewarded and that could educate her up through university. But she didn't see the money.

"Put a stop to it," I told her, but then I remembered that I should ask her her name and when I asked, she said proudly, "What will my name mean to you and do to me? Go away."

Afraid that she could scream and accuse me wrongly of what I didn't do and the persons attracted by her screams would cause my arrest and thus spend some days in custody before the truth would be known, I moved on or away. Saddened, but with hope that when I told the future queen, she would do something about it, I mentioned it to Godsheren.

And her reaction: "I will stop it. It will not be seen or heard that there is paedophilia in Godsheren City. Unfortunately, the children of this generation don't look downwards at the ground or walkways to see and find diamond pearls or obstructions and avoid bumping into them. Additionally, they don't look horizontally in front of them to see whether they will bump into a human or an electric pole planted in the ground. Their looks are focused on the smart devices they hold in their hands, looking neither to the left, or right, downwards or horizontally ahead of them or upwards. In this way, they miss what Earth can offer them. And also, what the sun or the moon or the waters can offer them through the power of sight.

"The 'lost' youngsters are my priority. You can't live in the queen's subjects' residences, built with flower gardens in front of the houses and orchards at the back, and handed to parents free, and do what that seven-year-old was doing. All they should be doing is tending the gardens with any child from age of five (teaching them to appreciate flowers and orchards and the importance to every family), and, additionally, to pursue a career or find employment to earn monies to feed their children and themselves and pay only for water and light. No such will happen in Godsheren's realm. And if any parent should fail to do that, then the parent is not fit to live in the kingdom. And any children of theirs must become the queen's children to live in the queen's houses (one) to be built in every suburb of one hundred residences (sub-counties).

"There is one country in a desert area that my parents told me about. The women are hardworking, trustworthy, neat and respectful, and would add value to whatever you give them . . . innovative is the word. I will instruct that that country's women be granted 'Shepherd' visas to come and work in the queen's houses. I am certain that the women from that country won't want to go back to their country. And we will then convert their status to subjects with all the entitlements due a subject of the queen," Godsheren explained.

"Alternatively, their country could become part of the unified kingdoms that will come under you?" I suggested.

"If the men would prove themselves in qualitative terms as their women, that would be excellent. But otherwise we accept all the willing women," Godsheren mentioned.

"Hmm! That is a direct destruction of that country. Because a country with no women or only a few would fight each other to death, and cease to exist," I said advisedly.

"It is the policies of a country's leaders that determine flow of emigration. I doubt if there will be any emigration from Godsheren's kingdom," Godsheren explained.

"We could travel to that country soon after your coronation, to confirm what your parents told you, and to be sure that they haven't become like others who detest work and therefore live in squalor and poverty?" I suggested.

"Eh! My mind, eyes and ears have daily followed events and happenings in that country. It is a virgin and fertile country to recruit from or simply establish a diplomatic mission in and issue as many women the Shepherd visas and cover all costs of relocation and settlement," Godsheren said.

"Wow! Building a kingdom, maintaining it or expanding it, all involve strategic thinking and tactical measures so as not to falter," I said.

"That is the conclusion of the matter. And that is why some fail and others succeed. I will succeed, not only because of strategic thinking and tactical measures, but because I have the four goddesses behind me to lean on, for defending and attacking," Godsheren said.

CHAPTER 20

THE QUEEN'S DAYS FOR VARIOUS BODY TOUCHES AND THE SMILE DAYS

Jacksonville, FL, USA
August 11, 2018

An aunt of Godsheren paid us a visit when our thoughts were on various strategies and tactics to employ to reign for the good of the subjects. And she offered no mean advice when Godsheren mentioned about various days to be set apart as queen's days for various types of body touches.

She said, "A mother nursing a baby knows when her child is sick because her body is always in contact with her child. The mother will therefore seek treatment for the child to restore him or her to health. And so also must a husband and the wife's bodies touch frequently every day so that when one of them is unwell, the other will know and advise that treatment be sought.

"Furthermore, when it is a matter of stress-induced tension common in men, an attentive wife will proactively act by 'seducing' her husband with sexual relations, instead of waiting for the husband to ask. And most stressed men don't know that it is lack of sex that causes most stresses and therefore tension in men. And where even the stress and therefore the tension wasn't caused by lack of sex, but hard work or long hours of traveling without rest and no good sleep (to help partially), the sexual act will give immediate relief."

When she was finished, so we thought, with what she had to say on body touches, she showed us a video.

There was a man in the video who had worked all week long, was tensed and was chatting with four women about headaches and body aches, and the women asked him to take pain relief medication and he would feel great again. Into the room walks the wife, and she asked the husband to sit on a chair, and he did without the four other women who were in the room hearing or seeing what was about to take place. She, in a long dress, sat on the husband's lap, with the dress spread out so that his body could touch hers. She unzipped his pair of trousers and said, "I am your wife. I will lift my butt off you a little. Go in." He ejaculated into her four times and there was such a sudden flashing relief in his body that he loudly asked (followed by deep breathing by him), "Ah! How did you know this is what I needed, when I didn't know?"

His question aroused the other four women, who asked, "What is happening?"

And the man's wife responded, "He is relieved of stress associated tension."

The four women, not having seen what happened and still not seeing a wife still seated on the husband's lap, (because both were covered with darkness but not currently in a romantic posture), took leave of the man and his wife.

"That is the end of the video: a true-life story. I use it currently to teach the technology generation of what can be done by women to keep men bound to women. But I am not done on my pieces of advice on the topic of various body touches. But if you have any reactions?" Godsheren's aunt asked.

"We have done it that way a number of times. It makes you go crazy and be really in love. Boo, do I speak for you?" Godsheren asked.

"Oh, yes! And I have reacted most times like the man in the video. Aunt, I hope you didn't secretly record Godsheren and me, and has redacted our faces?" I asked.

"An aunt is a mother. And a mother doesn't record the daughter's sexual moments for any purpose," the aunt responded, with a smirk on her face as if to say, *I wish I could live those times again and also relive them through the brain recollecting those moments, for those warm and enduring for hours sensations.*

"Well, the next comment on body touches. Parents and their children must touch each other by appropriate touches. Hugs are highly recommended. You'd know if anyone is unwell instantly when you hug them. And not to forget to give friends a hug; or even strangers a handshake.

"Therefore, in the matter of the throne, since all subjects are members of the kingdom and of the queen, a back rub from the queen on them elevates them to your level in their minds, though you are still a queen, with their daily chorus of, 'Long live the queen'."

"Auntie Balana, thank you. A hug for you," Godsheren said and hugged her. "And so the days of every week will be set apart as follows: hugs and kisses among nuclear family members every day. Also, every day, will be smile day to and for everyone in the realm. Additionally, among friends, hugs and back rubs as appropriate. And finally strangers, a handshake and, as friendships develop, body touches as appropriate," Godsheren mentioned.

"Against such an edict from the queen, none will kick, except those who wish to live lonely and miserable lives," I said.

"I wish you well in your preparations, Godsheren. And you, Boo, also," Aunt Balana said.

CHAPTER 21

FIRST ANNIVERSARY AND THE UNVEILING OF GODSHEREN'S PARENT'S TOMBS

Jacksonville, FL, USA
August 12, 2018

We arrived in Godsheren City seven days before the date for the unveiling of my parent's tombs. I couldn't tell who gave information to the various groups or clans of people who came to welcome my husband and me and gave gifts of various eatables, sufficient for us, my aunties, nieces, cousins, uncles, nephews and the members of the visiting clans or groups. It was the custom that a visitor to your home was not hungry at home, but you must share your meal with him or her or them, for a visitor who refuses to eat or share the same meal with you has an evil intent and that would prevent him or them from eating your meal.

And therefore, in accordance with custom, the first clan that came on Sunday following the Saturday of our arrival waited for a meal to be prepared, and it was prepared out of what they brought. I didn't know how my nieces and aunts did it; but while we were still receiving the felicitations of each member of the visiting clan, a period of about forty minutes, they came to inform that the food was ready. Those who will eat boiled sliced yam ate boiled sliced yam pieces with green leaf tilapia stew. Others, I didn't know, had opted for the baked sliced yam pieces (a case of, my conscience is clear and I will eat in your home and put in the request – good for those who don't like things to be done differently from how they liked), with ground fresh pepper and baked grouper.

Others ate ewoakple (corn powder cooked and moulded into balls and eaten warm, traditionally, not ever when it cools), and 'fetri detsi' (okra stew made from fresh okra picked from the farm that day's morning, cut up into thin slices, with spices and smoked salmon cooked).

Have I accounted for the different dishes but all under one meal, lunch? Oh! Yes, some others ate 'dzenkple' cooked with smoked shrimps, anchovies and boiled salted salmon, palm oil, peppers, tomatoes and corn powder. I ate a little of each dish, but not too much to be full and throw up causing offence to those who cooked, for it would be explained that it was because the food was either not well cooked or tasty, hence my stomach rejecting it. For a future queen must not offend or cause offence to any subject in her dominion, lest the subject be ever worried that not having pleased the queen, his or her days could end at any time. No king in the past, from my reading of the kingdom's history, ever detested any subject in the realm as to make the person worried because the person failed to please in one way or the other.

My love, Boo, copied me in the order I did things that day. But he soon complained of hunger, as my portions to him were 'soon to be a queen's portions'; a queen who will help herself with eating from at least three hundred thousand women's kitchens on special anniversary days, and will take minute portions of each woman's dish.

There was a surprise for us. The surprise, because it was not expected, was that the visiting clan members took turns to each sing and dance (but no drums were involved and therefore no beating of drums) to possibly tell the future queen that when you need a member for an orchestra, a choir or traditional singing and dancing group, remember me or him or her. Well, it was a joyous, with many hours of lunch and recreation and not tiring.

While my husband soon felt hunger pangs, and had hoped that only one or two would sing and dance to represent all of

93

them, so that a niece or an aunt could get him something additional to eat, he 'gave' his thoughts fully to the singing and dancing. And that way, his hunger pangs ceased. That was what he told me when we had our showers later in the evening and retired to bed.

Sleep that night was good, as we both heard the songs sung earlier that day in our memories, and maybe we dreamt of what happened earlier in the day. And that was a fit-full replacement for him and I being ensconced together in romantic love.

In the morning, he mentioned that, "Ah! The mirth associated with singing and dancing is quite an alternative to sexual relations between a couple, but not perfect. And therefore, I will still cast the ballot in favour of sexual relations."

And to his statement, I responded, "Then sexual union between a man and a woman is more powerful than the queen's power."

And he replied, "And more than the power of a king and all kings and queens combined. Make a law against it or issue an edict and your kingdom will be in flames. And so please, Queen Godsheren, on your coronation encourage them to do it."

"Such an edict will be against yourself also. Or will you exclude yourself? I need not an answer. It is unreal. And will be surreal. The king or queen's kingdom will end that day, and the king or queen will be no more such, all the subjects committing suicide," I said.

"I'd love to read or hear one such law before leaving Earth to go and live life in the waters," Boo said.

"Oh! Oh!! You have forgotten that there was no such law passed – a universal law – but kings had eunuchs in their palaces. I don't know their reason. But possibly so that such eunuchs (men) would not have reasoning capacity of the awesome kind. Because the sexual act, when performed in a mutually satisfying manner, increases the power of reasoning. I will do no such to anyone as queen; for none will have the brain capacity I have, and which I will use daily to transform their lives and kingdom with no burdens on them. A challenge only rises when you impose burdens on your subjects," I explained.

The next day, the king came with his counsellors when we had planned to pay a courtesy call on him and his counsellors in the palace. We welcomed them with open arms and warm smiles, because you don't drive a king away from your house because he has broken protocol that was designed for his honour, you accord him respect and protection.

They brought vegetables, fruits, palm nut oil, varied foodstuffs, poultry, and fishes, but no four-footed animal. And while the young men were slaughtering the poultry and cutting them up, the women cleaned the fish, cut them, and soon the aroma of different dishes blew into the living-room, with the king and counsellors sniffing the air – evidence that when it comes to food, there is neither king or counsellor or subject. All are equal then.

There was joviality in our conversation those few hours before lunch. There was no evidence of a king or counsellors among us. But our conversational words to each other were decorous and respectful.

Then the king, after looking at wall clock opposite him indicating the time, said, "The food must be ready. Because when men are hungry, then the food is ready for eating."

"I will go to the kitchen to check," I said, and stood to go.

And the king again spoke, saying, "The different dishes should be served in large glass bowls so that we can all serve ourselves from the large bowls."

"At your service, King," I said.

"Godsheren, you are not being fair to me. When we are to eat together, close your mind to a king been present," the king advised.

"Yes, Uncle," I answered.

"That is better," the king said.

When I returned some fifteen minutes later, with sixteen women carrying different sizes of glass bowls containing different dishes, it laid in the mouth of the king to speak again, saying,

"When you smell the freshness of cooked food with your nostrils, know that the food is not only from freshly harvested fresh produce and freshly caught fish or poultry, it will also be tasty, and when you burp as you eat, the odour is fresh as morning glory flowers. Not the same with frozen foods of all kinds."

When I rose to give a plate to him, he said, "Not that also." And he stood and took a plate and a set of cutlery, and took a little of three dishes as a first course. Others also did. And I was priest to pray over the food. The counsellors, however, started eating earlier than the king. He and I, coincidentally, put the first bunch of vegetable salad picked with the fork into our mouths at the same time.

"I taste the freshness of the vegetables. In our home, we ate fresh foods every day, because my parents were poor and couldn't buy a refrigerator and freezer for storage. And we harvested from our garden or bought each day with whatever money Mother, after putting her right hand under Daddy's thigh, would get. And we didn't leave any food over till the next day, also in accord with our clan's prohibition on its members not to eat yesterday's or, appropriately, the past day's food," I said.

Counsellor Letsu spoke for the first time since they arrived with the king. He praised my parents for not eating 'dead food' that was many years ago cooked food and was frozen and, when needed to be eaten, re-heated for feeding her with.

"We thought we were modern, had moved with the times because we had money and bought refrigerators and freezers for storage of foods. But, in that, we were worse off than the poor, who ate fresh foods daily, some only once a day. Because the fresh foods I ate today," – by this time they all had eaten the three-course meal – "had a taste and freshness one hundred times better than cold stored foods I ate in a year.

"We expect that, after your coronation, new edicts will be issued for the good of the subjects, and some of us will live life like the poor, eating fresh foods or freshly cooked foods daily. I belong to the same clan as you. But my wives cook or reheat the three-year-old already cooked frozen food and freeze them to be eaten over weeks because, to them, the kitchen isn't only for wives and if I wanted freshly cooked food from fresh items every day, then as a human being I should also go to the kitchen. Also, as far as they were concerned, already cooked frozen food was handy and a great time-saver," he said.

"Hmm! I wish lightning would strike one of these days and take out every fridge and freezer in every home. And, unable to store frozen foods, we would walk the ancient paths of cooking and eating freshly harvested or caught food items," Counsellor Danlu said.

When the clock chimed at four o'clock in the afternoon, it sounded louder than usual, and they all took it as a polite advice by an artificial object to them to leave, and they departed from my parent's home.

Other clans and some of their members who called on us on subsequent days, and did the same things as those before them did, were the Adzovia, the Bate, Amlade, Bamee, and Dzevi.

The first anniversary and tomb-unveiling took only an hour. It was a solemn ceremony, and the remaining clans to make the total number of fifteen clans were in attendance. After the ceremony, they went home with us and, like others, they offered gifts as those before them, and they were prepared and cooked and everyone present ate. Their dance groups also performed, just as members who were singers.

And before dusk, when they all left for their various homes, we felt the spirit of loneliness descend on us, though we were more than forty-eight relatives still in the house.

"Oh! There is joy in numbers. And every home must boast of hundreds, so that the kingdom in boasting of hundreds of millions will be a joyous kingdom, because all will share with none hungry, all will sing and dance to drum beats or songs, with none excluded," Boo stated.

"Was that a prayer?" I asked. "Yes, amen," I then said, answering my own question.

CHAPTER 22

THE CORONATION DAY OF GODSHEREN AS QUEEN

Jacksonville, FL, USA
August 10, 2018

On the night before the coronation, there was joy, laughter and smiles on faces of some two million people out of the three million inhabitants. The youth were out in the streets celebrating what would be a new future for their city and kingdom. They had seen the mounted light poles at one hundred-foot intervals but were not aware that the tastiest healthiest water was going to be part of a new future on the coronation of the queen.

But a little after midnight, the heavens opened and rain fell so much that by four in the morning the drains were filled and overflowing. Instead of rain aroma associated freshness, the air stank so much that most sleepers woke up and continuously sprayed perfumes and air fresheners in their rooms. By five in the morning the rain had stopped, and different flowers fresh scents kept blowing in homes and outside homes.

But a few of the king's counsellors, eight out of the twelve, met and decided that a royal family male member should be crowned as king and not Godsheren, whom the king had abdicated in favour of. Their reason: the heavy rains and the many hours of long offensive odour. They met the abdicated king and the three prospective royals (who had all deferred that a queen on the throne would build up Godsheren City and kingdom into a true kingdom) informed them that a male royal must be crowned to reign and gave their reasons as such.

The abdicated king then asked them, "Do you still smell the offensive odour? And is the rain still falling?"

"As far as our noses are concerned, yes, and we are still breathing in the offensive odour. And this has not happened in the city and kingdom in the past. Please, royal family, don't destroy your kingdom by giving it to a non-royal. The signs are there for you to know that her kingdom will stink to the high heavens and all the people will perish. And a kingdom without subjects is not a kingdom but a family on their own, that is if you also don't die from breathing the offensive odour."

"My sons, what air are you breathing? Stinking air or the aroma of different flowers?" the former King Giteza asked his sons.

"Oh, Daddy. The aromas of different flowers and sweet-smelling trees. And each aroma definitely has a meaning for the future, and that only can be greatness of our kingdom, and therefore sweet-smelling, to bring more into the kingdom. Those who are not smelling the freshness and the sweet smells or aromas are not destined to be part of the future and of the kingdom," the three answered.

"What my sons have described is what I am smelling. You should go away so that we can prepare to be at Godsheren's coronation as queen," he said, and stood up, and the eight counsellors walked ahead of him to the doorway. And they, on looking ahead of them at the sky, saw the moon and sun as if they were merged, whereupon all eight said, "Another strange event of nature. It is a warning!"

"That is not true. It is rather the opposite. The sun and moon are happy about the coronation of Godsheren as queen. Have you not seen that the earth, that had so much rain a few hours ago, has dried up for the ceremony in four hours' time?" the past king said.

"We can't be part of the coronation with all the warning signs from nature. And it is we, as counsellors, who understand the times and seasons by our knowledge of what nature or part of nature says or does and interpret it to the king for successful reign. But you have now spurned our advice. So be it," the eight counsellors answered him.

"Oh! The kingship was mine. The throne is for the Giteza royal family. And we have given it all out to another – Godsheren. Is it the fear of losing your position? For every king may maintain or pick others as counsellors. And for your not understanding the current time, (through the signs of nature), you have lost your position. Bye, no more from you," the past king firmly said, retraced his steps, and got ready with other royals for the coronation.

The royal family members were seated at the rostrum on what were called 'the royal's grounds' some thirty minutes before the first blast of the trumpet, that lasted thirty minutes, to signify that there would be a new royal procession. This was followed by the royal marching song of 'New Queen, New Queen' three times, singing, 'All hail the new queen, all hail the new queen' three times, and the same words till the new queen was seated for the ceremony to begin.

Sixty-two women aged sixty-two years, each in glistening white long dresses (the envy of the angelic hosts who wear white always) with pots of water on their heads, dance-walked into the grounds. They were followed by fifteen fifteen-year-old girls carrying lamps and, as the first stepped out of the room from which they were dressed, the sunlit sky darkened till all fifteen were seated.

A third group were sixty six-year-old girls in purple dresses, accompanied by two chaperones, and they carried baskets of various fruits and vegetables in either their right hand or left hand, such that thirty carried it in the left hand and thirty in the right hand.

The group of sixty six-year-old girls was followed by twelve persons, consisting of six males and six females, dressed in the uniform of the various services that operated under the previous king and the additional services to be introduced by the queen.

In all, ten new services professions were to be introduced. They took standing positions, unlike the first three groups. Then, seven trumpeters blew their trumpets, and there appeared Godsheren's carriage with a mounted cavalry of seventy men and seventy women on white mares (horses) leading the carriage. The procession moved at the walking pace of the horses, none looking left or right but straight ahead. And with twenty more steps for the first two horse-riders to enter the grounds, everyone stood up, and as the fresh sweet-smelling flowery scents were blowing at and on every one, nobody in the history of coronations (and there had been six in the past, including that of the only king to abdicate: King Giteza) used the artificial fans most carried to fan themselves.

The royal announcer, after Godsheren and her attendants sat, called for the ceremony to begin, each allotted five minutes to do whatever he or she must do. The archbishop said the opening prayer. The announcer then introduced the former king and a few monarchs from other kingdoms, who had been invited to witness the coronation of a queen but who would serve as king, not that she was married to the king to be his queen.

King Giteza recounted the history of the past kings and said, "It has pleased the goddesses to give the people of Godsheren City and kingdom, a queen."

At that, instant rain showers fell in front of the rostrum and the sun, as if it had a message from the moon for the queen, appeared directly above only the rostrum, other locations suffering brief darkness. The past king thereafter helped Godsheren to stand, and she recited the vows; and the past king and wife put the diamond-studded crown, with seven doves engraved in circular formation, on her head. And he declared, "Godsheren, you are Queen Godsheren from this day and forever." There was rapturous applause as the air was filled with more of the sweet-smelling flowery scents.

Queen Godsheren gave a brief speech as follows: "I am your queen from today because I knew poverty, not that I could not have known riches also. But I desired and my parents also desired that for me. But during my reign, I will know riches with you and share the riches with you all. Everyone is of the kingdom and makes the kingdom. And all those who desire to be under Queen Godsheren, I will share my life and reign with. I salute the four goddesses. Thanks to past kings for creating and maintaining the kingdom. Thanks to the sun, moon, the waters and the Earth."

Then was it that the kingdom anthem, modified was rendered, namely 'We Have a Queen', was sung and, when it ended, the subjects started clapping as food-packs in bowls with the queen's name and coronation date on it dropped from aircraft, and everyone had enough as the number of members in his or her family. And there was the further instruction that a bowl food-pack could be taken and given to a non-family member who couldn't be part of the ceremony.

"Long live Queen Godsheren" they shouted as the queen's carriage left accompanied by the cavalry and followed after by the other groups.

Hours later, there was beating of drums, singing and dancing in the twenty counties of the Godsheren kingdom till late at night, and the sweet-smelling scents carried by the wind didn't cease that day, a reminder that the goddesses when they are reigning through an approved queen live among the them (subjects) and the aromas are the indicators of their presence.

The following day's news items had varied headlines: 'The Kingdom of Aromas', 'The Kingdom of Fresh-smelling Wind', 'The Goddess's Kingdom', 'Queen Godsheren's Kingdom'.

CHAPTER 23

THREE MORE KINGDOMS
UNDER QUEEN GODSHEREN

Jacksonville, FL, USA
August 13, 2018

It was after breakfast, one Monday, that Godsheren said to me, "My intuition tells me that three kings from the three nearby kingdoms will come to make certain demands and I will refuse them."

"Hmm! Intuitions also play roles in the affairs of kingdoms?" I, Boo, asked.

"Yes, for those who have intuitions. And no for those who don't have intuitions. As the days go on, you'll get to know what other sources you can get knowledge from in keeping and maintaining your kingdom," Godsheren answered.

"And when they come, what will be my role, since you'd expect me in the meeting?" I asked.

"For this first year of my reign, while observing and learning through experiences, you'll keep a faithful record of whatever I will say and decisions taken and whatever they will also say. That is a recorder in long-hand. For kings and queens don't use modern gadgets, they could be hacked," Godsheren answered.

"Please, queen, will I be introduced as such – a recorder?" I asked.

"You make me feel sad. Why use the word 'please' for me? Are you not, firstly, my husband and, secondly, being given the role of a recorder? I will introduce you as my husband and a recorder. When we married, I was Godsheren, without title or a crown of a queen. And that comes first. Know that you will be a husband and I will be your wife Godsheren, not Queen Godsheren," Godsheren explained.

"I sincerely apologize. I am glad the husband and wife relationship takes precedence over the queenship and the kingdom," I said.

"Have you taken a look at the sun today? Towards its eastern part or quadrant with its melancholy look? This simply means the sun is sorrowing over some nations; no, it is the three kingdoms that are in that quadrant," Godsheren said.

"I didn't notice it. I will go and take a quick look now," I answered.

"Oh! After our early morning walk through the gardens, we stepped out into the palace courtyard, at my request, and I looked up for a while. I thought you also looked up?" Godsheren asked.

"Yes, I looked up. But because I didn't know the sun could communicate, I took no notice of its features then," I explained.

"You must from now onwards be particular with regard to the four goddesses," Godsheren advised.

A cold sweat broke on me and my heart missed a number of beats. But fortunately she was being informed by one of the female courtiers (from the protocol department) of the arrival of the three kings then.

"They have come, as I anticipated. We must go to meet them in the Crown Meeting Room. I know their demand and therefore the meeting won't go beyond one hour. Get the necessary support staff to be on hand. You have done that in the past, when King Babanbo and his counsellors came over," Godsheren mentioned.

With all protocols observed, Queen Godsheren asked what demand they wanted her to comply with.

The three kings' spokesperson, King Lassu, said, "Your Royal Highness, since your assuming the throne of the Godsheren kingdom, we have known no peace in our kingdoms. Our subjects have with their eyes seen the infrastructural projects your kingdom is carrying out at night on royal land abutting our borders. We desire that Your Royal Highness take immediate steps to build a sixty foot-high by four foot-thick wall to screen your developments from the eyes of our subjects, and also prevent our subjects from entering your kingdom to cause insecurity. Your Royal Highness, that is our plea. Let it not sound like a demand."

"Your Royal Highnesses, I have listened attentively to your spokesperson and the demand being made on me and my subjects. I am unable to accede to your demand. A king or a queen secures his kingdom through good policies, to maintain the loyalty of subjects, but not by another royal obstructing their inalienable right to move elsewhere that he or she or they could be welcomed.

"I am securing my kingdom by infrastructural projects in all counties and sub-counties of my kingdom. I will furthermore expand the kingdom and, like what you have seen being done at night, kings or queens must work at night while subjects are asleep, so that by the morning, they (subjects) will know that they have a caring mother, in the case of a queen, and caring father, in the case of a king.

"We will not block our subjects' right to air blowing from your respective kingdoms to mine, or vice versa, and free movement from my kingdom to other kingdoms, unless those kingdoms place restrictions on entry of my subjects, and vice versa," Queen Godsheren told them.

All three stood up, bowed and asked to leave. Her Royal Highness saw them off to the palace courtyard and bid them well.

A month later, the protocol department forwarded a letter, signed under the hand of the three royals, requesting that they wished to merge their kingdoms with the Godsheren kingdom, and renounce any right to any throne, as that was the only prudent course. Failing which, their subjects would overpower the various royal families in the three kingdoms, kill them and destroy any history on them, and merge with a kingdom that offers them, not only hope, but reality. It mentioned that their subjects had even noticed the 'Yamefe' (sky houses) being placed in the sky as alternative dwellings should the ground be ever flooded by the sea on one boundary of your land.

Queen Godsheren signed and sealed a response that I wrote to them as follows: 'Her Royal Highness, Queen Godsheren, respects your decision, but desires that your subjects affirm her as queen over them on specific days when Her Royal Highness's ambassadors or special envoys will be in your kingdoms (which shall cease to be your kingdoms from the date of affirmation of Queen Godsheren) to supervise the subjects' affirmation.'

On the dates communicated by them to Queen Godsheren subsequently, she sent envoys to supervise the affirmation. Hours later, because all three kingdoms chose the same date for the affirmation, the subjects came in droves to the Godsheren kingdom's 'crown one million field' and asked to see their queen.

Godsheren rode on horseback with the cavalry of the kingdom, and, with their loud shout of, "Long life to our Queen Godsheren!", three kingdoms were added in a day, to increase the number of subjects to one hundred and eighty million.

That night she didn't sleep. She met with construction project executives to plan massive infrastructural projects in the newly merged parts. I also didn't, as I sat to her right, very observant not to miss one word or a sign or symbol from her or any other.

After the queen's breakfast with all these executives the next morning, they bid her well and promised to complete the various infrastructural works in six months.

CHAPTER 24

QUEEN GODSHEREN'S CONSCIENCE MOVING ON STEEL STORAGE TANKS OR FUNDS

Jacksonville, FL, USA
August 14, 2018

It was at a lunch with the one thousand infrastructural constructional contracting firms' executives (and after eating her five-course meal), that Queen Godsheren said, "I have kept faithfully to the contract terms with each one of the firms that you are chief executive officers of. But some of you have not kept your side of the bargain. I have discharged all financial obligations to you. You recall that in your contracts, you are (I mean the firms) required to turn over all precious pearls recovered, found or won to the queen's treasury. But that has not been done. And just a day before my sumptuous lunch with you, 787 of the contracted firms have recovered one form of precious pearl or the other. I know all the different types of pearls recovered. . ."

She paused and scanned the faces as if she would mention the firms and their chief executives by name. Five minutes went by in a conscience-imposed silence around two particular sections of the large hall where the lunch took place. It seemed the 787 chief executive officers were put in those particular sections. The unaffected in the third section were chatting among themselves

After a tense fifteen-minute pause by the queen (still on her feet), she asked, "What will the affected firms do in compliance with contract terms?"

A hand shot up. "Yes?" the queen said.

"Your Royal Highness, I wish to speak for and on behalf of my firm".

"Speak," the queen said.

"Your Royal Highness, my firm found or won diamond ore, but I and board members were under the impression that we ought to hand over polished diamonds and not the ore."

"Was that what was in the contract?" Queen Godsheren asked.

"Your Royal Highness, you cannot present unpolished diamonds to the queen, he said, and he slumped to the floor. The queen's aides rushed to his side and started doing CPR. A cough was heard, but they carried him away for further examination.

"It was his conscience that wouldn't allow him to speak untruth, that was why he collapsed. It was an untruth-induced heart attack. I pray he makes it," the queen said.

Then another hand shot up from the section where the chief executives chatted earlier, when the queen spoke about 787 not complying with the contract terms.

"Yes," the queen said. "You wish to speak. Speak," the queen said again.

"Your Royal Highness, I am Renou Ballast, chief executive of Many International Limited. Our firm didn't find, win or discover any precious pearls. We would have handed them over. My firm has been in the construction business in many countries and kingdoms for over forty-five years. When you dig deep enough in some locations, the ground offers many prized pearls. But most national leaders and royals, actually two thirds of countries and kingdoms, don't have that provision in their contracts. Regrettably, some firms think such pearls are perks for digging."

"Well said, Mr Ballast," the queen said, and smiled broadly, and Mr Ballast smiled at her in return. "I could give you an hour to chat among yourselves to come up with what the 787 firms will do," the queen suggested, and with no answer she retired from their presence.

Mr Ballast moved to the two other sections (the silent sections), and said, "I am not going to accuse anyone. But I know that when we do wrong things, they do haunt us with imposed silence. If the queen knew the number of firms at fault, it means she knows other details but doesn't want to disgrace anyone. The defence or excuse put up by our colleague didn't help him, and you saw the result. The queen has rightly explained the incident, and she is no ordinary mortal from what is going on in her kingdom. Please, restore all to be in her good books. And then every project in her expanding kingdom will be ours."

All the 786 heads in the banquet hall then nodded their heads in agreement, possibly afraid that opening the mouth to speak could mean the use of the wrong word and mishap might befall the speaker.

When the queen returned an hour later, she asked, "What was the decision arrived at?"

Mr Ballast stood up and said, "Your Royal Highness, everything will be restored. We don't desire any more mishaps."

All in the two silent sections clapped simultaneously and were followed by the third section in no synchronized order.

"I take that to be unanimous consent for what Mr Ballast said on your behalf. It is easier to lodge all the pearls in whatever form in the Conscience Moving On Steel Storage Tanks or Funds. You will find them at your various sites. When one gets full, it will move away and another tank will take its place. You are welcome to take part in an afternoon cocktail before going away. Thank you," Queen Godsheren said.

CHAPTER 25

QUEEN GODSHEREN'S FIRST ANNIVERSARY
ON THE THRONE

Jacksonville, FL, USA
August 15, 2018

The queen, at a meeting with her counsellors (they'd rather listen to her counsel), informed them that she was disbanding the royal police service that was set up by the first king and had existed during the reigns of the five others. And for the first time, the counsellors objected, saying that this had not ever in any kingdom or nation been done, that the kingdom or nation wouldn't have a security service that would protect life and property.

"Your Royal Highness, we must vote on this matter and, please, the majority vote, with respect, should override the queen's powers," they said.

"Then you are the queen. I will be justified to dismiss all of you, before disbanding the police institution whose head has written to resign and asked that the numbers be reduced. You have his report. Have you read it? And followed the queen's law of reflecting on matters before speaking or asking questions on it? Are you working for what you are earning? You don't think being idle most times of the day without using your brain, or labouring on a farm, could reduce your life expectancy?" Queen Godsheren asked them.

With heads bowed, they said, "We each apologize for suggesting voting. Your Royal Highness is right in what you desire to do. If the head of the police service wishes to resign because there is no work being done by him, and he is earning a salary from the realm for very little or no work done, and because his conscience has pricked him, then it is good for the realm that he resigns. Those who leave the realm's service could catch fish from the seas or the lagoons or perform at other careers or professions."

"You are aware that, since my coronation, no crime has been committed and those who have caused any damage to properties of the realm have paid into the Conscience Fund and given their personal details – details that the edict setting up the fund stated were not necessary. I will ask all police personnel to resign and therefore look for other vocations. I am likely to ask you also to resign in a couple of months, but before my first anniversary. He that rues his or her conscience ruins his or her sleep," Godsheren explained.

"We have been having sleepless nights since your coronation, unlike during the reign of King Giteza. And we didn't know it was because we were taking undeserved salaries and therefore rued our consciences with the sleepless nights. Your Royal Highness, we will cast nets into the sea for fish six days every week, for 'he that struggles with the sea (monstrous at times and serenely beautiful at other times) preserves his physical and mental health'."

"Your position as counsellors you will maintain in a ceremonial capacity. If and when other subjects see your examples through work, none will play 'Sipa' (the card game) all day under the shade of coconut trees, while eating their wives' meals at the day's closing, having not toiled. They will join you or relocate out of the kingdom to where people only play games but eat.

"In my kingdom, the conscience spear will strike at them one by one. You have the evidence of that in the queen's services. It is not only the police that will be affected, the judiciary will be affected by voluntary removals too. And the chief judge has been in contact. Some, I will appoint as envoys; others must use their brains to do something else. Only two will be retained at the high court level – the court of first instance. Three judges to sit and determine appeals filed (the Court of Appeal; the final court of the kingdom) will be paid based on cases adjudicated on," Godsheren said of the future."

Coincidentally, just a month before the queen's first anniversary, the royal forests, parks and garden service employees ceased to sit in their offices six days a week but started working in the queen's residences and houses, occupied by subjects and children respectively, to give advice and to make their hands dirty. They teach the names of flowers, plants and trees, dos and don'ts to justify their salaries, as if they know that the queen will reduce their numbers, or scrap them also, and hire private companies to do the work as and when needed, and be paid based on actual hours put in (industry).

The queen, impressed by their proactive response to the changed circumstances, will give them during the anniversary the 'Queen Godsheren badge of honour for proactive service'. Others will also be awarded. But not the one thousand contracting firms who adopted one thousand sub-counties, and whose letter to Queen Godsheren twenty-eight days before the queen's first anniversary, read: 'Your Royal Highness, Queen Godsheren of the Godsheren kingdom, warmest felicitations from the one thousand contracting firms working in your kingdom. It has pleased us to adopt a sub-county each. And each firm from the date of this letter will be responsible for maintaining all health, educational, cultural and recreational facilities in the sub-county of its choice. Respectfully, find attached the sub-counties and each responsible firm.

We note we don't pay any form of taxation in your realm. And we ought to reciprocate that by indirectly paying back to a kingdom that permits us to use its roads, harbours, and others, including social services, without a dime. Long live Queen Godsheren.'

It was signed by the hand of one thousand contractors. And upon the queen's instruction, a response was sent to them to acknowledge their kind assistance.

But just a week to the anniversary, another letter was received from the firms stating that each of the thousand wished to relocate their international headquarters to the Godsheren kingdom. They also offered to underwrite all costs associated with the first anniversary celebration.

And just a minute after midnight, of the day of Queen Godsheren's first anniversary, the sweet-smelling aromas of flowers and trees that daily blow throughout the kingdom became three times in intensity, and woke up most subjects, and they got out of bed and started singing and dancing in their residences and houses.

"Not ever has a day for the celebration of king's anniversary in our realm brought in sweet-smelling whiffs of fresh air. The goddesses and nature are celebrating our queen's anniversary. And what can us mortals do, except to sing the queen's praise, the praise of the goddesses and of nature. Thanks and praise to Queen Godsheren. Thanks and praise to the goddesses. Thanks and praise be to nature," were heard from the queen's residences and houses.

Incidentally, before commencement of the formal activities related to the anniversary, there was a heavy downpour of rain for one hour. It was followed by the sun rising at 5:30am with a hotness that was never felt in the kingdom, and it dried the water-soaked land. But the subjects were unmoved, knowing that nature in its various forms were also celebrating a queen that they played a role in crowning. That hotness lasted thirty minutes. The hot sun then became cool, with temperatures ranging from 18 degrees celsius to 22 degrees Celsius, depending on what each subject would be comfortable with, so as not to take a sweater to keep warm or a fan to keep fanning to keep cool in the body.

And, as 8:00am struck, the children from the queen's homes, with their 'shepherd mothers' from the desert country, walked to music sung alternately by three traditional singers. They were followed by the royal cavalry, and the queen was heralded by the blowing of the seven trumpets that must always herald the queen's arrival. The queen's anthem, entitled, 'Royals Live Forever' was played by the Queen's Royal Band.

Next was a mass orchestral performance by twenty thousand subjects. And the queen, in a regal pose, looking forty and in an angelic white long dress that sparkled, gave a five-minute speech, the essence being, "You are no more subjects of the realm and therefore of Queen Godsheren, but sons and daughters of the queen . . ."

The queen's badge of honour was then awarded to 1,578 sons and daughters by name.

A while later, each royal naval vessel (sixty-three of the five hundred) in the kingdom sounded a bugle for a minute, as sixty-three aircrafts (which could be converted for civilian use by pressing a knob) of the Royal Air Force flew over the grounds.

Two hours later the ceremony ended. And sons and daughters were directed from their own homes to spend seven nights in another's home (the greatest movement of people in any kingdom or nation with enough ships, aircrafts, coaches and trains and teams involved). But that was done after the sponsored lunch by the one thousand firms had been eaten. And as each arrived in their new location or residence, music was played in every room in every residence or house in the kingdom, and that continued non-stop for the seven days, with the continuing whiffs of sweet-smelling flowers and trees more pronounced (three times more) than ordinary days in the year.

And so it was that on returning to their own queen's residences and houses (though each was the queen's), they all buzzed the queen's secretariat with the words, 'Your Royal Highness, we desire the music playing in all rooms to be part of our daily lives, whether it be night or day. Signed, Respectfully, your children.'

And the queen granted their petition and it became customary that music played in every room in every residence and house in the kingdom every moment.

CHAPTER 26

A FIFTH KINGDOM COMES UNDER
QUEEN GODSHEREN

Jacksonville, FL, USA
August 16, 2018

We were into the third month of Queen Godsheren's second year on the throne, when she mentioned that a fifth kingdom contiguous, (with a population of seventy million people), their king and ten others from his palace would be visiting us to ask questions about the best practices on maintaining a kingdom, developing the welfare of its people, and building or updating infrastructure.

"Wow! Seeking for best practices from a queen who has barely been a year on the throne, a few months ago? I thought best practices were learnt through experience, and therefore would be taught by kings and queens who have reigned on thrones for decades?" I, Boo, the queen's husband, asked her.

"When you hear, see or read about great infrastructural developments and health and wellbeing of subjects, crime-free, increased life expectancy, cooking and eating fresh food or produce every day in a particular kingdom – matters that haven't been addressed in any other kingdom past or present – it is humility of heart that will make you ask for best practices from that royal," Queen Godsheren explained.

It was on the agreed date with the Royal Protocol Department that the queen and a few others, including the queen's husband, met King Lingado and his entourage. This was an hour after hosting the visiting royalty a choice breakfast prepared when each made a request to ensure that the ready food came crisp and crunchy, and the palate felt the freshness of the grilled, baked, fried, broiled or roasted breakfast items.

The visiting king at the meeting said, "Your Royal Highness, no doubt change, unquantifiable change, has occurred in your realm in terms of physical development, and in the lives of all the people within your dominion without discrimination of any sort. How were you able to do it? And is any other king or queen able to do it? I ask this last question because of the fresh whiff of sweet-smelling aromas of flowers and trees blowing through your kingdom every day. We use artificial preparations bought. Yet a few with flower gardens in their homes have the benefit of the sweet aromas."

And Queen Godsheren responded as follows: "If you are an exceptional monarch, the elements of nature help in your exercise of sovereignty–"

"With respect, Your Royal Highness, it is not for a monarch to interrupt another monarch when that monarch was speaking. But your beginning words disqualify us from being monarchs. Could we put in a petition to be merged with your kingdom, as we know you have kindly done to other kingdoms? My subjects and I will become your subjects. For it is the wise who sees or notices something happening in another kingdom and cedes his kingdom and its subjects to the superior kingdom, and continues to live rather than for the subjects to overthrow the king, killing the king and the royal family in their desire for a better life as in the superior kingdom," King Lingado implored, and those with him nodded approvingly.

"Your Royal Highness, King Lingado, as much as it would please my children in the Godsheren kingdom to have others be part of their kingdom, it shall be that your subjects must affirm me as their queen. And when that is done, you'll become part of the Godsheren kingdom, initially as subjects, and to rise in status to become children – that is, sons and daughters of Queen Godsheren," the queen said.

"If it pleases, Your Royal Highness, Queen Godsheren, we will promptly take leave and return and do what is expected of us." King Lingado removed his crown from off his head and said, "Your Royal Highness, you are my queen. If it were not for the task ahead of us, I would not return to my kingdom, and would have made history as the first king who sought a better life in another kingdom," King Lingado said.

A week later, with the affirmation ceremony concluded and Queen Godsheren their queen, then the population of the Godsheren kingdom rose exponentially to two hundred and fifty million, with a land mass bigger than the biggest continent.

CHAPTER 27

QUEEN GODSHEREN WANTS EVERYONE TO KNOW WHAT IS HAPPENING IN THE KINGDOM

Jacksonville, FL, USA
August 17, 2018

The queen said, "My husband, Boo, boyo boo, I have every five days of the week, after romantic hours with you, left home with my two female aides (they also wake up from the bed on which they sleep with their respective husbands), to spend a total of three hours with the contractors who are carrying out various under the ground projects for the realm. And I have returned to find you still deeply asleep as you were before I left you. It will have to change when my two aides are in the sixth month of their respective pregnancies. You will have to be by me then."

I was stunned that the sexual acts gave such deep sleep that wives could leave their husbands behind on the matrimonial bed for more than three hours every day, for five days of each week, without the husbands realizing their wives' absence. And the more I thought about what she said, the more I became afraid of the sleep-inducing power of sexual relations on a man. I felt that a wife who was in love with another man could give a husband contented sex that would make him fall into the deep sleep associated with it, go away to the lover for three hours, and return with a commission from the lover to thrust a dagger through the husband's heart, and if she did, you would die in your sleep thinking you were having a dream of a death thrust by means of a dagger in respect of another man.

"Eh! Boo, boyo boo, I spoke to you. Did you hear my words? You didn't react in any way to show that you heard me," Queen Godsheren said, and it was then I realized that I was lost in thought for many minutes.

I therefore said, "You deserve tons of apology. And I offer that in hugs to you. Seven hugs that feel and feed your body, and yours, mine." I did.

Then she said, "I hope that also doesn't send you sleeping for hours? But you have five more months yet to sleep deeply, for they are each one month pregnant."

"Goal Godsheren," – I also had coined a name for her – "I will go out to work with you at night for the three hours of those five days each week, and after be queenly rewarded with what puts men to sleep deeply for the remaining two hours of the new day," I answered her.

"Sexually contented men sleep better. And the reason I have allowed you to sleep is for you to carry Queen Godsheren's burdens – personal and that of the realm – if for any reason I decide to take a few days' holiday. Then you will live on the memories of those sexual times and deep sleep times without a complaint in your heart," Godsheren explained.

"Oh, queen – the word 'queen' in small letters – you have forewarned me. Love extracts the greatest sacrifices and equally offers the best returns. And you have given the greatest sacrifices. It now falls to me to give the best returns and to even extract the greatest sacrifices again. It is a circle that must not be broken," I said.

"What I had wanted to tell you is that, from now on, you will ensure that all in the kingdom know about everything the queen does; however, not the underground works done at night and her presence at some project sites deep at night. I will do that on the various project's commissioning dates. Additionally, what is happening in each of the queen's people's residences and houses with regard to those living therein to others, and vice versa, I wish to know, and each also knowing events or happenings in the realm," Queen Godsheren said.

And so it was that I designed a queen's information flow page to all in the kingdom with two hundred and fifty millions people's pages to the queen.

When my first communication from the queen went out about the establishment of the queen's page for information from the queen to her children (subjects), the response was overwhelming. There were 247,899,123 responses (word for word) as follows: 'The information flow from the queen is unnecessary as we have practical evidentiary materials through our eyes, ears, nostrils, tastes and feelings of what happened pre-coronation and post-coronation and continues to happen every day. Please, what even we cannot discern with our five senses, we will in due course detect with the five senses. Things being done underground are not detectable by the five senses. Did the queen not construct and install water systems from the rocks underground when she wasn't as yet a queen? When the works were being done, nobody detected with the five senses that water of the best kind was what would be flowing through taps across the kingdom. Your works, oh queen, will continue to speak for you. They are renewed every day because you are a faithful queen.'

And when I read the same type of response from the millions to the queen, she shed tears of joy and said, "Their responses are not human responses drafted by humans, but whispered into their ears by the four goddesses, hence the consistency. A kingdom that depends on the natural elements will not ever fail, for the natural elements were timeless and are timeless."

She knelt down on the diamond-encrusted floor, raised both hands, and mentioned the four goddesses by name. She then got up and asked, "What things are they saying among themselves? For when you don't hear what your people are saying, whether it be for good or for evil, you don't have a 'mirror' to speak to you about your works."

"Oh queen, the word 'queen' again in small letters, I am yet to collect that data and convert it into compact information. I will use the next one week for that, my darling wife," I answered.

"Eh! Your using the words 'darling wife' or is it 'daring wife' imputes something to you and imposes an obligation on me, not as a queen but a woman," Godsheren said.

"If it pleases and arouses the passion in you, yes. And in celebration of your people's response," I answered the queen or the woman in her.

"A few hours later, then. For if all the people praise you, but you don't have a 'him' near you to celebrate with you, you are but a spirit posing as a human in a human world," Godsheren answered.

Two hours later, the queen said, "Queens can defer hope without making the heart sick, but a woman who made a promise to a man of sizzling touch cannot defer what was hoped for. It makes him sick."

She undressed and I, for the first time, appreciated her reference to 'but a spirit posing as'.

She cuddled me, as I also did her. And there was mutual ecstasy, for she moaned repeatedly, and it turned into deep breathing such as I have not heard from her in six years as we laid on the floor, and I also simultaneously sang her praises as a wife. Next, when the good demons that entered us left, we showered.

When a queen is faithful in great things (sacrifices), things of the realm and of marriage, you must be faithful in the little things. With that at the back of my mind, I collected the data on what the people (children) wrote about the changes they had had since her coronation, and began the tedious work synthesizing. Men work better from the 'restorative' effect that comes from sexual acts. And in four days, I had synthesized two hundred and fifty million-plus responses on the following as listed by the people:

1. Rains at least twice every day before dawn and after dusk, watering our gardens, cleaning or washing the minutest dirt on the walls of our homes in the queen people's residences, including our cars and anything that was in the way of the rains

2. Our harvesting fruits and vegetables from our own gardens each day, eating those fresh fruits and vegetables every day or, where it is too much for one family, giving it to the neighbours, who may not have enough, or whose fruit trees have not started yielding, so that every home has everything, except how you cook yours from others.

3. Coordinated vegetable planting at different times, so that there is all-year-round availability of fresh vegetables for everyone and no one has to freeze any, and for fruits, too, to ensure that the harvest is at different periods for different households so that, again, there are fresh fruits all year round.

4. Continuous music in the queen's people's residences and houses; and continuous blowing of the aroma from flowers and trees.

5. Examples of hard work by counsellors emulated by the youth from every family.

6. The cohesion among one family and therefore among all families in the realm, such that none are envious of another family

7. The practice of walking through each family's two gardens at morning and in the evening, speaking to the plants and flowers.

8. Elements of nature playing roles in the lives of all the people in the kingdom.

9. Visitors or strangers not mistreated or cheated.

10. Good and refreshing sleep.

11. Physical developments of public parks, swimming pools, recreational facilities – namely theatres and cinemas – and refresher courses in colleges and universities free of charge.

When I briefed the queen with my synthesized data and therefore informative, her face lit up. But she asked, "Are my children becoming lazy, because natural elements have taken on some of their responsibilities?"

"No, not in the least. None desire to die. They are more active the next day than the preceding day. Their attitude (boys and girls, men and women) could be summed up in the following sentence: 'Where and when nature intervenes to do what I did, I looked for something else to do physically and mentally, so that nature would not become like an intelligent (artificially intelligent) robot to replace me on Earth'."

"They have taken on the nature of their queen. The leader of nation or kingdom determines the nature of its people," Queen Godsheren said.

"Oh! It stands to reason why some kingdoms fail, while others succeed and even expand," I said by way of deduction to her.

"Your deduction hasn't gone far. It should include many others, such as institutions, firms, schools, colleges etcetera," Queen Godsheren said.

CHAPTER 28

QUEEN GODSHEREN, FIVE YEARS ON, TEN YEARS ON, AND SILVER JUBILEE YEAR ON

Jacksonville, FL, USA
August 18, 2018

Queen Mezzom of Lolunda kingdom's welcome dinner ended at 9:30pm. And when she was about to retire to one of the palace's guest dwellings in the royal forest, the aura of which was unmatched in any other kingdom because of the different singing and talking trees surrounding the dwellings, Queen Godsheren pretended to kiss her and wish her goodnight, but rather said to her, "Queen Mezzom, you will have to change from your royal robes to a dress fit for subjects (children they are called in my kingdom).

"In my kingdom, there is only one class. There is no lower class, middle class or upper class. I and my husband wear clothing with the crown's jewellery and a few other outward adornments for only distinguishing purposes but not because we belong to a different class.

"I will spend the nights and days that you are present in my kingdom with you in houses of my subjects (in my kingdom referred to as children), and we will start that tonight.

"My ladies in waiting have three suitcases full of different dress styles, blouses and skirts, and kaba (a woman's long dress sewn as one piece) for the thirty nights and days away living with and among my people."

"Oh! What a surprise!! I had thought of making the request to spend nights and days with your children. But the advice my counsellors gave was that it would amount to my undermining Your Royal Highness, Queen Godsheren, if it was something you hadn't done in the past. Wow! I am all for it," Queen Mezzom said.

"I have not slept outside the palaces in residences but it is something I have planned doing, and therefore waited for the opportune time. And that turns out to be your royal visit," Queen Godsheren explained.

When both queens were done changing, an aide dropped them off at the nearest sub-county interchange.

Each queen had a suitcase with a travel tag on, and hand luggage that they easily pulled on the walkway.

And it was about 11:00pm when Queen Godsheren pressed the buzzer to a residence where the lights were on in all their rooms – an indication most likely that they were not asleep. She turned to her guest and said, "It is required of guests wishing to spend a night or nights in any family's home to give truthfully their first name but not titles. And additionally, whatever the host or hostess offers you upon your entry to the home, you smile before receiving it and also smile after receiving."

When the outer door opened, a woman stood in the doorway in her nightie and said, "Welcome to my queen's people's residence and my home," She stretched her hand and took the two hand-sized suitcases and further said, "Follow me."

When we entered and sat down, she said, "There are two rooms available for the night, and possibly for however long you wish to stay to finish with the business that brought you. And if you are a mother and daughter, and you wish to use one room so as to chat the night away before falling asleep, your pleasure will be mine also."

And while she was yet talking, a teen girl brought two glasses (mugs) to each of us, filled three quarters full of a drink. I smiled and took the two glasses offered to me. My colleague did likewise.

We drank half of what was in each glass mug and, noticeably, Queen Mezzom accurately echoed whatever I did.

Then she asked the question, "What are your names?"

"I am Godsheren. And my sister is Mezzom," I answered.

"You carry our queen's name. She is an exceptional queen. And your voice sounds like her. Were it not that queens don't sleep in their subject's home because of protocol and safety, I would have hugged you as my queen and your sister. I will still hug you before bedtime. My husband is asleep. I am sure he hasn't turned the lights off in the bedroom before falling asleep, so I will have to do it, a difference between him and me. Another difference between us also relates to sleeping time. He sleeps early and I always afterwards. That should be the only thing that separates a wife and a husband in the Godsheren kingdom.

"Oh! I am sorry. I should show you to your rooms on the first floor. My daughter will bring along your suitcases, one after the other. And please, when you are settled, I will fix you a dinner of herbs and protein and a mug of beverage of your choice. The veggies and protein are from our garden. My apologies. I am Martha Mator. My daughter is Angula," Martha said.

It took us twenty minutes to get by before we descended the staircase downstairs to the dining room, next to the kitchen and living area, and our nostrils picked up the inviting aroma from the food, different from the aroma that nature gave the kingdom daily since my coronation.

We had a light dinner and chatted for some fifteen minutes. Then we left our hostess for our individual bedrooms; but not before she hugged each of us tightly, so much that we felt the warmth and love of her hugging – the type of hugging that must be the norm in homes with a husband and a wife, and extended to their children and the children their parents.

She asked also that just before sunrise we could join her family for a walk through their two gardens, a fruit tree garden and flower garden, if our bodies permitted.

When Queen Mezzom and I retired to our rooms, my room being closest to the couple's bedroom, I overheard her wake her husband up, who asked, "Is it on tonight? You have withheld it many nights already."

And she retorted, "What about the daytime ones after all those nights? Don't they count?"

"Are you keeping a record, my sweet wife? The nights are longer than the days, and you can shorten them with contented sexual relations and deep sleep thereafter," he said.

Why are they talking at the top of their voices and thus making me hear what I shouldn't hear? I asked myself. It was after my self-questioning that I heard, "I am hosting the queen. Please, nothing tonight."

"What? You must be crazy or dreaming? If dreaming, that is permissible, but a mental case, let it not be," her husband answered.

"Okay, we are hosting two women. One is called Godsheren. And the other Mezzom," she responded.

"Oh! It is her name that makes you conclude that you are hosting the queen?" he asked.

"More than that. Her voice sounds like that of the queen. And my intuition tells me that it is the queen. I have found favour with her in a special way. Ever since the two entered into our home, the intensity of the diverse aromas that the wind carries or blows on us every day have increased," she answered.

"You could be right on that, because since her coronation awesome things have happened. But that applies to all in the kingdom. Maybe the increased intensity is because it is a special day in her life and therefore in our lives. Sweetheart, anyway, if the queen is in our house, let us make it a home with a goodnight kiss, followed by goodnight hugs. That will be in order, and celebrating the queen's presence. And don't tell anyone lest our house be overrun," I heard the husband tell the wife.

And fortunately I didn't hear anything else after the husband's admonition because tender sleep took me to slumber-land for four continuous hours, which when I woke up from was as if I had slept for twelve hours. But then, a thought flashed through my mind: what if queens, though humans, never slept? And the thought of it, and possibly a yes to it, made me shake violently. The saving grace was that Mezzom buzzed me about our hostess's invitation to the 'life' in the gardens in the morning, and I assured her that we would be part of it. And we did.

Martha introduced us to the husband before our walk and our conversation among us and with trees and flowers began.

We, after the garden-related issues, and after a quick shower, went to the kitchen to help Martha prepare breakfast from garden-fresh ingredients. We ate with the couple and their daughter, Angula.

We (Godsheren and Mezzom) went for a drive for two hours with our hosts. They mentioned the great achievements of the queen by pointing out landmarks to us, and we expressed appreciatively our 'wows', 'awesomes', 'excellents', 'ahs' and 'ohs', among many others.

We noted that whereas Martha was always looking closely at our faces (incidentally partially covered with a headscarf), the husband did no such.

We returned home to cook lunch, and after eating with our host family, we excused ourselves to go and do some writing work of a few chapters. And that elicited a question from Mr Mator. "Oh! You are both writers?" he said.

"Yes," we simultaneously answered.

We spent a total five nights with our first host family. And as we were leaving, to go elsewhere for a night or more stay, we offered each member an item of clothing that fitted perfectly, and when husband, wife and teen daughter tried their respective shirt, long dress and blouse and skirt on, they said, "Unbelievable that you knew our sizes and colour choices!" one after the other, starting with the husband or father.

Tears welled in their eyes as a palace car, disguised as a chartered car, came to a stop outside their gate. A handshake from us to Mr Mator was all he got. And women being women, we hugged each other fondly, as if we had known ourselves personally for decades and had not seen each other for some years.

When our suitcases were tucked into the car trunk and we opened the car doors and sat down, Mrs Martha Mator said, "That definitely is Queen Godsheren. For it is with her that exceptional things are associated."

And to her statement, I, Godsheren, said, "You will sleep in the palace some days before my fifth anniversary. But your daughter, Angula, will spend her next school holidays, two months away in the royal courts."

"Oh! How awesome!!' Mother and daughter said, and ran into the residence still in tears.

After Mr Mator bowed in reverential manner three times, he closed my car door, did the same for my companion, and we drove away.

Queen Mezzom and I spent the next twenty-five nights in twenty-five homes. And except for four, where only husbands were at home and hosted us (because their wives and children were away elsewhere in the kingdom), the wives in the rest of the homes recognized me as Queen Godsheren. They were also invited to spend time at the palace in like manner as Mrs Mator.

And so it became known that the queen could pay you a surprise visit to stay in your home, and therefore there was the daily expectancy of the queen's visit, and a home ready to receive her visit and your reciprocal visit to the queen's palace.

Queen Godsheren celebrated two decades of anniversaries, each with its innovative things before and leading to the anniversary, such as the invitation of men to stay in the palace for a defined period, for the reading of select books and discussion of them with the queen's husband, who earlier had also read those books; and for playing 'Ampe', a game involving at least two women, solving riddles, puzzles, and alphanumeric word formations or numbers, and other games, with the queen.

When Queen Mezzom returned to her kingdom after Queen Godsheren's silver jubilee anniversary, she told her counsellors that, "When subjects are expectant of their queen's visit to a subject's home, the home is kept like the queen's palace. Further, when subjects know that they could play games with the queen, or discuss books they have read, or will be asked to read and discuss, they will prepare six times over in readiness. And no mind or hands, feet or legs or arms will be idle in such a kingdom, and the kingdom prospers and it is also safe."